DIAMONDS OF THE NEVER NEVER

DIAMONDS OF THE NEVER NEVER

RICHARD W. HOLMES

&

RANDY L. HUGHES

Author website: www.ridgewater.com

Illustrations by Boris a.k.a. Bryan Cook

Website: BorisCarArt.com

Acknowlegement

My thanks to Connie Rothwell for her encouragement and support.

To my Australian friend, Kevin McNaughton, who told me stories and took me to many places in Australia that most Australians have never seen.

Haystack Creatives
8270 Woodland Center Blvd
Tampa, Florida 33614
www.haystackcreatives.com

ISBN: 978-1-953115-60-7 (sc)
ISBN: 978-1-953115-68-3 (e)

Library of Congress Control Number: 2016948548

CONTENTS

We dedicate this book to the memory of all the family members whom we loved and left this world for a better place.

Books written by Richard W. Holmes

The Ratters of Lightning Ridge (2005) 1-933678-02-X

Kate's Capers in Cumborah (2006) 1-933678-11-9

The Diamonds of Jaruk (2006) 1-933678-13-5

Ben's Revenge (2008) 978-1-59948-159-3

The Ratters of Lightning Ridge (2009) 978-1-59948-208-8

Big River Turkey Farm (2011) 978-1-59948-322-1

Treasure Too Far (2012) 978-1-59948-392-4

Diamonds of the Never Never (2016) 978-1-59948-596-6

The **Never Never** is the name of a vast, remote area of the Australian Outback, as described in Barcroft Boake's poem

"Where the Dead Men Lie":
Out on the wastes of the Never Never—
That's where the dead men lie!
There where the heat-waves dance forever—
That's where the dead men lie!

CHAPTER 1

KATE AND RUSTY'S TRIP TO SYDNEY

Five years have gone by since Kate and Rusty found the forty diamonds in Jaruk's back yard, took 38 of them to Sidney, and locked them in a bank vault for safekeeping.

* * *

Yeah, Rusty, it's Kate. Say, let's meet at the Blue Light Café at 8:00 for coffee." Kate listened to Rusty. "Look, I'll tell you when we meet. We have a problem. I'lltell you then." Kate quickly hung up the phone and heard her dogs barking outside her cabin.

Kate ran out the door to see what the ruckus was about. "Hey! Shut up! Get over here," she growled at her three kelpie dogs as she caught sight of the rear end of a wild black hog running through the bush. The dogs didn't need to see the

boar. With their acute sense of smell, the dogs had no difficulty picking up scent of this foul smelling animal. While Australians hunt and kill wild boars, Kate did not want her three kelpies getting involved with this boar with no protective collar or front breast plate to protect her dogs from being torn up by the tusks of the wild boar. Hearing Kate's calls to them, they quickly retreated to her side. Kate's control of her dogs was the result of herding sheep and cattle in the bush. Kate's snapping at her dogs came from her irritation from thinking about what she must discuss with Rusty in the morning.

* * *

The next day, Kate drove to the café and parked her ute in reverse, as is the custom in Lightning Ridge. Rusty was getting out of his fifteen year old red ute. You could tell from the many dents, scratches, and cracks in the windshield that it had seen better days traveling through the bush.

Rusty touched the brim of his Akubra hat in Kate's direction in recognition of her presence. Kate and Rusty said nothing to each other until they sat down at a table in one corner of the restaurant.

"Gee, Kate. It's been a while. How are things?"

"Ah, running sheep and chasing cows. Let's get some coffee and maybe some grub. Hey Sue! Our usual, but coffee first." Kate, in her usual rough way, shouted across the room to Sue, who was half way through the room, making her way to Rusty and Kate's table. Sue, who was use to Kate's rough way, turned around and headed for the coffee pot and a couple of cups on the counter near the heated coffee sitting near the kitchen door.

"Well, Rusty, you know I'm not for a lot of words. I like to get right to it," said Kate. "Yesterday, I got a letter from the Westpac bank in Sydney where we put those diamonds. The letter says we haven't paid the lockbox fee in five years, and under banking rules and state regulations, they have the right to open the box and clear it out. The letter goes on to say that we have sixty days to pay the delinquent fees, or they will confiscate anything in it."

"Wow Kate! I guess we better hightail down there and clear it out," said Rusty excitedly.

"Yeah, you know it takes both of us since we did a duel signature thing—neither of us trusting the other one. This time, let's split up the loot and be done with it. Since we sold two diamonds out of the lot that means nineteen for each of us."

"How do you suggest we divide them up?"

"I thought about that, too. When we get the diamonds, we'll flip a coin and sees who goes first and gets first pick. Then the other fellow can have the second pick until we each have half. I see no other way. Neither one of us has had anything to do with diamonds as to know their quality and value. I don't think at this point we want a third person looking at them. So, let's just split up the loot and take our chances with our choice of stones."

"Yeah, Kate. Sounds fair to me. I'm getting low on funds. I haven't had much luck finding any good opal lately. I would certainly like to sell some of those diamonds."

"Now wait up, Rusty. Let's don't get ahead of ourselves. Remember what Steve Saunders said about selling raw, uncut diamonds. We got lucky selling those two stones to the two strangers that Steve lined us up with. I'm not sure what Steve will have to say about what we do. You know it has been five years since we met with him. Once we pull the stones out of the bank, we can go see Steve. I'm sure he will still be in business down at The Rocks in Sydney. That's all he does is make and sell jewelry."

"Hey, Kate. What ever happened with those six stones Ben found after we dug that eighty foot hole out at Allah's Rush?"

"I buried them in a tin behind my cabin." "Don't you think we should split up those too?"

"I imagine so. Divide up the lot. We did share in drilling that well. I paid Ben ten thousand dollars, if you remember, to get him to give up his two stones. I think it's only fair that I keep four and you get two of the six stones."

"Well, alright, you did put up the money for his stones, and I didn't have any to square up the find. That's fair. However, since you are keeping four stones I think I should be able to pick out my two."

"Oh, alright. Who knows what any of them are worth?

I'll go along with that."

"How and when do you want to go down to Sydney?" "I would like to get this out of the way. I have everything under control with my sheep and the cattle. They all have plenty to eat right now with the recent rain. I wouldn't mind leaving in the morning. You got anything going?"

"No, Kate. Not really. I'm not on to any good opal right now, and the mine is all locked up at Mulga's Rush. Not much activity out there either. Everything has been rather quiet. Even some of the mates who I know who are on to opal aren't digging. The demand for opal seems to be down right now. There is plenty already available in the market, and no one is buying. Yeah, I could leave tomorrow. You want to drive?"

"Rusty, is there a choice? Your old rust bucket would only make one hundred miles down the road. We'll probably only get halfway down as it is a two day trip. Maybe we can stay at that same motel as we did five years ago—that's assuming it's still there. It seems like things change everywhere. We'll just have to see how it goes. Since we got a long way to go, why don't we leave tomorrow at 6:00? You can park your ute at the far end of the Bowling Club parking lot. Everyone knows your truck. No one will bother it there. They will wonder where you have gone. But let them wonder."

"Ah, here comes Sue with our food and more coffee."

* * *

The next day, as agreed, Kate and Rusty met at the Bowling Club where Rusty left his ute, and they were off in Kate's ute down the Castlereagh Highway to Gilgandra.

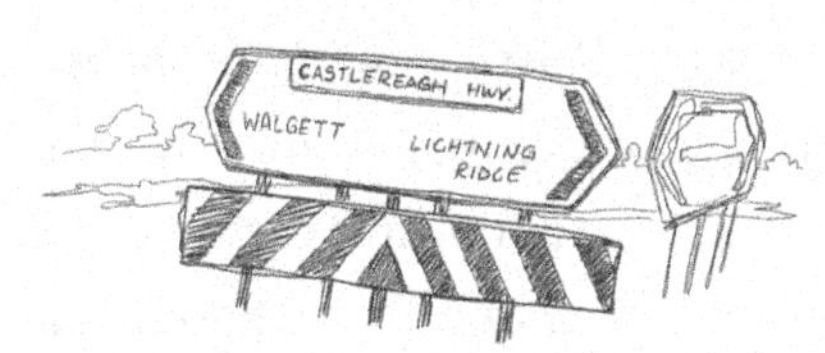

At Gilgrandra, they turned east on Highway 86 through Dunedoo, Mudgee, and on down to Katoomba. Kate had made this trip many times before, and she knew this route well. Another

driver might have chosen a different route to Sydney, but this was Kate's choice. Besides, this brought Kate to Katoomba where she wanted to stay the night.

It had been five years since both Kate and Rusty had been down this road. Both admired the change in scenery from the sparse bush country of Lightning Ridge to rolling hills of grass, sheep, and cattle pastureland as they got closer to Katoomba. They made good time and rolled into Katoomba about 6:00 P.M. The town had changed. The motel and restaurants had changed since they were there last. Kate did not like changes, and it unnerved her as they both looked for a place to spend the night.

Finally, they picked a motel that still had rooms available with a restaurant within walking distance. The motel was called Traveler's Rest, and Kate seemed more at ease once they had checked into separate rooms. The restaurant they went to was called the Boomerang

Café with a bright new neon light in the front window. While the café was fairly well filled up, Kate and Rusty were lucky to get a corner table where the previous patrons were just leaving. Rusty ordered two meat pies, a sausage roll, and coffee. Kate ordered ham, eggs, and coffee. None of the other patrons in the café paid any attention to Rusty and Kate, nor was another table close enough to hear what they were saying.

"Well, Rusty, now is probably a good time as any. I don't think anyone is watching." Kate slowly pulled a dirty brown pouch out from her pocket, containing the six diamonds Ben had brought up from the new hole Kate and Rusty had dug at Allah's Rush. Kate kept her hands cupped around the six stones on the table to hide any prying eyes from a nearby table. "Okay, Rusty, pick out the two stones you want, and let's get this behind us."

Rusty hadn't seen the stones since that afternoon that Ben brought them up from the mine. Kate could see his eyes get big looking at the stones.

In a low voice Kate said, "Now Rusty keep it down. Pick the two stones you want, and let's put them away. They are all about the same size. I don't give a rat's which ones you pick, so make it quick."

Rusty quickly picked two diamonds, and they both put the stones in their pocket. Both sat quietly and said nothing until their food came.

* * *

The next morning, Kate and Rusty were off by 6:30, having had their breakfast. Kate stopped at a nearby petro station to fill up with diesel fuel and check her oil. All seemed well with her ute, and the two of them proceeded on down Highway 86 on the west edge of the Blue Mountains just outside of Sydney.

"Boy, Kate, I can't wait to sell some of those diamonds! I need a new ute, new equipment for the mine, and maybe even some new clothes!"

"Hold on, mate. I told you we have to be careful about selling these diamonds. According to Steve Saunders, there are lots of problems getting rid of these stones. Like I said, opals, I know what to do and where to go with them. Let's hope Steve has some ideas and new information."

Rusty looked somewhat dejected by Kate's rebuff of his desire to sell diamonds right away. Little was said between them as Kate found her way into Sydney and down to The Rocks near the wharf in the center of Sydney. Both Kate and Rusty noticed different scenery from what Sydney had looked like five years previous. The parking ramp Kate had used was still there in the same location, much to Kate's relief. She parked the ute and walked to the nearby Westpac bank, where they had their lockbox with the thirty eight diamonds. Both looked with amazement when they entered the bank, as the whole lobby had been remodeled since they were there last. Kate looked at Rusty and mumbled under her breath, "Now I see why these bloody bankers want their money. Lots of new digs."

Kate walked up to one of the cashiers and said, "I haven't been here in a while, and we need to get into our lockbox we have in your bank."

The cute, small, blond teller with a bright pink blouse and dark blue skirt responded, "Alright, why don't you follow me, and I will take you to the person in charge of our vault."

At the counter for entrance to the vault, there was a short, heavyset, half-bald man in his fifties. Kate said to him, "We would like to get in our lockbox."

"Do you have your keys?" "Yes, here they are," Kate said.

Both Kate and Rusty pulled their keys from their pockets.

The teller looked down at the keys and the number thereon and opened his file folder for their number. The teller responded, looking up over his half-glasses, "It seems you are five years behind in your box rental fees. You will have to pay up those fees before I can let you into your box." Kate, trying not to look agitated and knowing that was what the man was going to tell her responded, "Yes, I know, I have a letter here, which I received a couple of days ago telling me we owe five hundred dollars. Well, here is your money."

"That's fine, I still need to see some identification from you to check against the signatures on the card."

Again, Kate did her best not to appear agitated and pulled out her driver's license, as did Rusty. Most of Kate's agitation came from the fact that she had always lived in the bush and did not like the city or city people.

"Well, everything seems to be in order," the teller said. "Follow me into the vault. I will get your box, and you can go to one of the private rooms to open it."

All proceeded well. Kate and Rusty took their box to one of the private rooms. Contained within the lock box was the little dirty brown bag with the diamonds they had left there five years earlier.

"Alright, Rusty, let's lay them out on the table and divide them up. I still have my bag in my pocket with the four other diamonds. I'll use that and you can have this bag for your stones."

Rusty had forgotten to bring a bag and had the other two diamonds loose in his pocket, so he was glad that Kate gave him the bag from the lock box.

"Okay, Rusty, you got a coin to do the flip?" "Uh, no, can't find one."

Kate looked at Rusty with distain. "Alright, I got one.

You call it."

"Heads," said Rusty.

The coin came up heads. "Alright Rusty, you're first pick," said Kate.

The process went very quickly with each obviously picking the larger stones first. It appeared that their choices resulted in an even split, even though both Kate and Rusty had no idea as to the value of any of the diamonds. The whole process took less than five minutes, and they were out of the room.

As they departed from the vault, Kate said to the clerk in charge, "We left the empty box in the room. We don't need it anymore."

The teller smiled at Kate and nodded in her direction in recognition of what she had said.

"It's 11:00. Let's go see if we can find Steve. I sure hope he is still there and in business."

Kate and Rusty walked down George Street near the Circular Quay Train Station and ended up in front of Steve Saunders' jewelry store, which appeared to still be in business. They entered the store where Shirley, who they had met five years earlier, was still employed.

Kate spoke first. "I don't know if you remember me, but we were here five years ago to see Steve."

"Yes I remember you. You're from Lightning Ridge.

Kate, isn't it?"

"Yes. Steve here?"

"No, he's out running an errand. I can call him on my cell phone and let him know you are here."

"Yes, would you please? We don't plan to stay in Sydney long," said Kate.

Shirley dialed her cell phone and told Steve that Kate was here from Lightning Ridge and would like to see him. She listened to Steve talking to her, then hung up the phone. "Well, it's a little after 11:00 now. Steve said he can be back here to see you at 1:00 P.M."

"That's fine. Rusty and I will go get something to eat and be back here at 1:00."

Kate and Rusty left Steve's store and walked over near the waterfront. Rusty said to Kate, "Hey! There's Rossini's, the Italian place. How about some Italian food?"

"Fine with me," said Kate. They both ate lunch at Rossini's, drank a lot of coffee, and watched the tourists go by, including the sightseeing boats docking, loading, and moving in and out of the harbor.

They were promptly back at Steve's at 1:00.

Steve was there when they walked in. "Hi, Kate. It's been a long time. I hope you brought me some fine opals? I could sure use some like the last batch I purchased from you."

Kate looked around to see who was there. Only Shirley.

"Ah, Steve, would you mind if we go in the back and talk?"

"Not at all Kate. Shirley has the store covered out here."

"As odd as it may seem, I don't have any opals for you this trip. Rusty and I had to come to Sydney and get those diamonds we locked up in the bank. I didn't pay the lock box fee for the past five years, and they were going to confiscate what we had in the box, if we didn't pay our fees. So we just picked up the diamonds and closed out the box."

Steve smiled and gave a small smirk. "I thought you would have gotten rid of them by now."

"No. You know we sold two to those fellows you linked us up with. We got scared off by what you said about having to report where and how we got those diamonds and the fact that the tax boys would be on our back, so there they have sat for five years."

"So, Kate, what do you want me to do about it? I told you before I don't get involved with diamonds, cut or uncut. Opal is my game."

"Yeah, I know. But can you give us any more insight about trying to sell them?"

"Look, I'm not in that business, and since you were here last I don't think anything has changed. If anything, the controls with that Kimberley process of reporting have gotten even tighter. At least that's what I've heard."

"So, do you think those two fellows we sold those diamonds are still around?"

"Kate, I didn't know those fellows that well. I haven't heard their names since you were here five years ago. Your guess is as good as mine as to where they are. I have had no contact with them. Sorry."

"That's a bummer."

"I can't even give you a lead as to where or who to talk to. Look, Kate, I have a meeting I must run to. Good to see you. Next time you're in town, bring me another parcel of high grade opal. Well, good to see you both. I have to run."

With that last exchange, they all got up. Steve went out the door first on to his meeting, and Kate and Rusty headed on their way back to the parking lot.

"I hate this place," said Kate. "Let's get back to Lightning Ridge and try and figure out what to do when we get back."

Since the day was half over, they decided to go as far as Katoomba, spend the night, and leave first thing in the morning.

CHAPTER 2

KATE AND RUSTY HATCH A PLAN

A week after returning from Sydney, Kate and Rusty were back for morning coffee at the Blue Light Café. "You know, Rusty, we can't let anyone in this area know we have all of these diamonds. They are still mad at the fact that they invested in that big hole out at Allah's Rush and got nothing for it. Whatever we do to dispose of those stones, we should only try and sell one or two at a time. Otherwise, the buyer will want to run down the price, since they know we have more diamonds.

"However, I have been giving our situation some thought. The Opal Festival is only a couple of months off. That fracas brings in a lot of outsiders with money. Also, some of the townspeople wished they had money to repair and do some upgrading to the community pool. You know those three diamonds are still locked up in the Mines Department safe, the big stone they found in Ben's hand when he died and the two, two caret stones found by Sir Collin Williamson when everyone was exploring the landscape for a possible dig at Allah's Rush. Rusty, I think I will go talk to Bill Higgins. You know he is still mayor of the town. I'm going to suggest to him that he should have the City Council approve selling those three diamonds at a public auction at the Opal Festival. Oh, wait, here comes Sue with more coffee."

"Don't you two ever get filled up from drinking too much coffee?" Sue filled both of their coffee cups, steam rolling off the pour.

Rusty looked up at Sue and smiled. "Nah, this is a good place to meet and talk over things before the day gets going. So, how are things with you Sue?" Rusty said, searching and trying to be friendly.

"Oh, I'm getting along. No thanks to you," Sue said, reflecting on her many advances to Rusty and his preoccupation with mining opal. Sue turned and went back to the kitchen.

Kate was glad that the conversation did not continue between Sue and Rusty. That was just old news. "Alright, let's get back to business. The mayor is coming up for reelection this year, so I think he will be keen on the idea of selling those diamonds and getting some free publicity. I can tell you for sure, that Gladys Hilts over at the Mines Department is such a busybody they won't even need to post the news. She'll have it spread all over town in one day."

Rusty, on the edge of his chair, listening closely to every word Kate was saying, started fidgeting. Kate could see Rusty was getting excited. "Now, Rusty, be calm. This is just one idea. If we are successful with an auction at the Opal Festival, we will both split up and find out the names of all the bidders on those diamonds. Then we can go back on the quiet and approach them to see if they would like to buy more uncut diamonds. That's the whole point of having the auction. It takes the attention away from us, but it may give us someone to contact to sell our diamonds. I could care less about those three diamonds at the Mines Department. I don't want to place any claim on them."

"Gee, Kate, you really have this one thought out. What about if we check the Melbourne and Sydney newspapers to see if we can dig up anyone interested in diamonds?"

"Yeah, that would be alright.

Here again, we got to go slow. We don't want to attract any attention. And you know people around here are really nosy about other people's business." Kate continued, "I got some other things to take care of in town. Maybe this afternoon I can see if the mayor is in. I'll catch up with you later, if I have any news. In the meantime, Rusty, keep your shirt on. If we don't handle this right, the whole thing could blow up in our face." "Yeah, Kate. You're right. See you later."

Both Kate and Rusty left the Blue Light Café and headed for their utes.

* * *

Later that afternoon, Kate was walking down the street to mayor Higgin's office when she fortunately found him on the street heading her way. With such an encounter, it didn't appear obvious that Kate was coming to see him.

"Well, hi, Kate. What brings you to town? We don't see much of you around here," inquired the mayor.

Wanting to appear cool and allusive, Kate said, "Oh, I came in for supplies. I had to meet earlier with Rusty to see if he could help me with moving some sheep later in the month. I can do most of the work myself with my three dogs, but once in a while I do need help. Say, mayor, what ever happened to those three diamonds the geologist had at that project back at Allah's Rush?"

"Gee, Kate, that's been a long time ago. I think they are still locked up in the Mines Department safe. Why do you ask?"

"Oh, I'm not interested in laying any claim to them, but this morning when Rusty and I were having coffee at the Blue Light Café, we couldn't help but overhear a couple of people talking about how the town might raise some money to repair the community pool and make some improvements. Seeing you, it just occurred to me that at this point I would think the city owns those diamonds. No one else can lay claim to them. Why not put them up for auction at the upcoming Opal Festival and maybe even get people to make additional contributions?"

"Kate, that's a great idea, but rather strange coming from you."

"Yeah, I'm not much into the town. But seeing you reminded me it was Rusty and I who got Ben down that hole at Allah's looking for opals, and he came up with a couple of diamonds, which we sold to a fellow in Sydney. Hey, mayor, it's your idea. I don't want anything to do with it. I understand you are up for reelection this year, and that might be a good feather in your cap. Look, mayor, good to see you; I have to be on my way. I've got to get back to my place."

"Yeah, Kate. Thanks for the idea. I'll bring it up with the City Council. I would think they would be all for that idea." "Again, it's your idea. Don't tell anyone I thought of it.

They'll figure I'm trying to get something out of it. See you, mayor." With that, Kate grinned to herself and continued walking on down the street until she didn't see the mayor anymore and returned to her ute.

The plan was set.

CHAPTER 3

THE ANNUAL OPAL FESTIVAL

As Kate had figured, the City Council went for her idea of a public auction for the three diamonds held by the Mines Department. Just as Kate predicted,

Gladys Hilts, the Mines Department clerk, eagerly spread the idea around town. The mayor even had an advisement put in the *Sydney Morning Herald* about the Lightning Ridge Opal Festival and a public auction to take place wherein three uncut diamonds would be sold. The news editor remembered the story about Ben dying in a cave in at Allah's Rush and re-ran that editorial alongside of the Opal Festival ad. As a result, a big crowd showed up at the festival with notice given that the auction would take place on Saturday at 2:00 P.M. in the parking lot of the Lightning Ridge Bowling Club. Mayor Higgins, not to miss this opportunity, was the auctioneer with Carter McDuff, the Lightning Ridge constable, and his deputy Kevin Stewart, holding the diamonds there for security.

It was 2:00 P.M., and all were assembled with the mayor standing on a raised platform erected specifically for the auction.

"Kevin, go sound the city siren telling everyone that the auction is about to start," said Carter.

The parking lot was full of people, with people on the nearby sidewalks and some even standing in the street. Kate and Rusty were in the crowd, separated and watching the crowd, as they had planned.

"Alright, folks, you all know we have had these three diamonds on display in the hall of the Opal Gem Show. To make sure everyone here get a look at them, we have displayed them in this Plexiglas box, which Carter and Stewart will carry through the crowd. We'll give this process about fifteen minutes, and then we will start the auction. I think you all know the story as to where and how these diamonds were found. I'm not going to go into that. The City Council decided since no one can lay claim to them, we are selling them today to raise money for the community pool that needs repairs, as well as some improvements. So, the money is going to a good cause. This is a cash and carry auction. If you don't have your money with you, you needn't bid."

It was a very pleasant day in late July, no rain, a slight breeze, and the sun was shining. As the mayor waited and Carter and Stewart passed through the crowd, people gawked at the stones. Both Kate and Rusty recognized the local people, but there were a lot of strangers in the crowd, some of which did not look too friendly.

"We are ready to start this auction. I am going to offer the small diamond for sale first. It is a bright stone, weighing in at 2.1 carats. As far as quality descriptions go, we leave that up to you the buyer. I will begin the bidding at one hundred dollars. Do I have any offers?"

Many hands went up, and the bidding proceeded in one hundred dollar increments, until the bidding slowed down at fifteen hundred dollars.

"Now, folks, you know this stone is worth more than fifteen hundred dollars," said the mayor.

With that, the bidding started again. It went to eighteen hundred dollars and stopped. "Alright, I will make three motions, and the sale will end. Going once, twice, three times. Sold!"

A big, heavyset man with dark features bought the stone. Kate could tell he was not from the area. He walked up to Carter, paid him the money for the diamond, and retreated to the back of the crowd.

"The next diamond is 2.3 carats in size and similar in color as the first stone I just sold. Do I hear a starting bid of five hundred dollars?"

Quickly from the back, the same man who purchased the same stone bid one thousand dollars. Everyone turned around to see who was bidding. The bidding continued up to nineteen hundred dollars, where the bidding stopped. Again, the big, dark-looking man won the bid, came to the front, quickly paid for the stone, and retreated to the back of the crowd.

"Now we come to the stone you have all been waiting for! This is the diamond found in Ben's hand when he was dug out of Allah's Rush over five years ago. It is a 12.2 carat weight stone. As you can all see here in the sun light, it is a very bright stone. I called Sir Collin Williamson from the University of London about this stone. Sir Collin said he remembered the stone, but they never kept any details about the quality of it. He did indicate that as a rough stone, it should certainly be worth at least one hundred thousand dollars."

A huge gasp went through the crowd about what the mayor had said about its value.

"I also contacted a couple of my jeweler friends in Sydney, who had heard about the stone but had never seen it. They said it all depends on how the stone is cut as to its value. But they too felt as an uncut fine diamond, it should be worth at least one hundred thousand dollars. Well, with that introduction can we start the bidding at one thousand dollars?"

Again from the back of the audience came the voice of the big dark man, "Five thousand dollars!" It was almost a roar.

Again, the crowd turned to see who made the offer. From the other side of the crowd, two small men, standing not far from Rusty, appeared to be making calculations, with one talking on a cell phone. They too were not local people. One man shouted out in a Mediterranean accent, "Ten thousand dollars!"

In the middle of the crowd, one of the more prosperous opal miners, who had been very vocal at the Town Hall five years earlier, Sam Waters, put in a bid, "I'll give you twenty- five thousand for that diamond!" He grinned and smiled at the crowd, sticking out his chest and looking rather important.

"You folks seem to have the hang of this," said Mayor Higgins. "Anyone else care to offer another bid?"

Again, the big, dark man from the back called out, "I'll give thirty-five thousand as my final bid."

A moment of silence fell over the crowd. The mayor waited for someone to speak. On the other side of the crowd, the small Mediterranean man with the cell phone raised his hand and said in a very low voice that few could hear, "Fifty thousand dollars."

Mayor Higgins replied, "Could you speak up a little?

We didn't get your bid up here."

In a louder voice, the little man shouted out his best, "Yes. I said fifty thousand dollars!"

Again, a hush came over the crowd. The local people could not believe that a bid would ever get this high. The crowd was silent, and no more bids were made.

"Alright, going once, twice, three times. Sold to the gentleman on the left with the cell phone. This was a cash and carry sale. We are done with this auction. Please come up, pay Carter fifty thousand, and the stone is yours."

With that, the crowd dispersed and returned to look at opals at the festival, which they all knew more about. After the two men got their stone, Rusty tried to corner them and find out who they were. They introduced themselves as gem cutters from Sydney. Rusty inquired if, at some other time, they would be interested in looking at some more uncut diamonds. They said they would, but they were out of money today, but to get in touch later after the Festival was over.

Kate, in a similar manner, tracked down the dark, heavyset man. Hereto, she inquired if he would like to see more diamonds. He said he would, but that she would have to come to his office in Melbourne. She got his name and address, and each went their separate way.

Kate and Rusty got together. Kate said, "Rusty let's walk over to the Blue Light Café and compare notes."

In the café, both Kate and Rusty took their usual corner table to be away from others. "Well, it was about what I expected. None of the local people bidding except Sam Waters, who always wants people to notice him. Other than his name and where he was from, I didn't get much out of that big guy from Melbourne. He seemed rather mysterious. His name was Nigel Smith. Rusty, what did you find out from those two fellows who bought the big diamond?"

"They too weren't very talkative. They claimed they were diamond cutters from Sydney. The fellow with the cell phone was Drago Vujic, and the other guy called himself Marko Tomic. I think they are both Serbs."

"Yeah, my guess too. The guy from Melbourne looked like a Russian to me. I don't know. I'm not into where people come from. Out here in the Bush everyone goes by their first name or a nickname. I guess if we plan to sell these diamonds, we'll have to know a little bit more about them. The auction idea gave us a couple of good leads. Rusty, we still have to be careful. If we contact these guys, we can only offer them a couple of diamonds, and don't let on we have any more than that. Otherwise, we will gather too much attention. We've got to be careful."

"Yeah, Kate. No worries. When do you think we can contact them?"

"We have to wait until they get back to their digs. Maybe in a couple of weeks. Look, I don't know about you, but I have to get back to my place. Take care of my dogs and checkup on my sheep. I'll check with you later. Rusty, I'm telling you, don't rush into anything quick, or we'll get into trouble."

"Okay, Kate. You've got good instincts. I'm with you." Rusty spotted Sue behind the counter, tying the strings of her apron behind her back in preparation of starting her shift. Rusty turned to Kate. "Kate, how about some coffee?" "No. I'm out of here, Rusty. Got too much to do." She stood, pushed her chair in, and noticed Rusty watching Sue.

"Rusty, not a word of this to anyone."

Rusty jumped, as if just pulled from a dream, and focused his attention on Kate, now realizing what she had said. "Huh? Yeah, sure. Not a word."

As Kate walked away from the table, Rusty turned his attention to Sue, who was casually wiping the counters, waiting for customers to begin showing up for the afternoon rush. Finally, Sue glanced up, noticed Rusty watching her, and smiled.

Sue slid around the edge of the counter, pulled her notebook and pen from the pocket of her apron, and approached Rusty's table, smiling. "What you need?"

Maybe it was because she had caught him watching her, maybe it was because she was smiling, even though she had caught him watching her, or maybe it was because he wanted to respond, "You," the question caused him to hesitate. He glanced around the room, weighing his options. While he was a smooth negotiator when it came to selling opals, he was rather slow in navigating other forms of negotiation, even those of the most mundane nature. Finally, he answered, "Coffee'll do."

"Um, ok." Sue tucked her pen and notepad into her apron without writing anything down.

She returned a minute later, unsmiling, with a steaming cup of coffee, a full pot of coffee, and an oven mitt. She sat the cup down, dropped the mitt on the table, and sat the coffee pot on the mitt. "Just keep the pot."

She turned away.

Rusty cleared his throat, "Sue?"

She turned toward him, wiping her eyes. "Anything else?"

Rusty cleared his throat, "You." It did not come out as decisively as he had planned, and in its lack of decisiveness, it sounded more like a question.

Sue answered, "No. I don't need anything else." She studied Rusty, who was now studying the table. She had seen him like this only once before, but she didn't want to let herself believe that his current state could be any true indication of his past actions. "Look, Rusty, hungry people are coming in. You need anything else?"

He cleared his throat loudly. A man two booths away from him turned and scowled, obviously startled.

"You," Rusty finally said, again, a little too loudly.

Sue said nothing, turned, and walked back behind the counter. Ignoring several customers who just walked through the door, Sue picked up a cloth and began mindlessly wiping the counter.

She was smiling.

CHAPTER 4

RUSTY HEADS TO SYDNEY

Rusty didn't tell Kate he was going to Sydney. He pulled out three diamonds from the tin can he had hidden in the ground behind his cabin at his Mulga opal claim, climbed into his old ute, and found the road they had always taken to Sydney, the Castlereagh Highway, to Gilgandra. When Rusty reached Dunedoo, his ute started to cough and bang and let off black smoke from the back of his tailpipe. Fortunately, just ahead on the right was an auto repair shop. Rusty pulled up to the gas pumps and shut off the engine. A mechanic covered in black grease came out of the door of the repair shop, scratching his head and looking at Rusty's ute. "Appears to me you got a little trouble with your engine."

"Yeah, you might say that. If I were home, I'd take it apart and see what the problem is. I'm on my way to Sydney. I don't have any tools. Maybe you could give me a hand, and we can figure out the problem."

"Sure enough. That's what I'm here for. Glad to help."

For the next fifteen minutes, Rusty and the mechanic poured over the engine. "Well, you're low on oil. You have a loose belt. This here filter is plugged, and I think you have one rod freezing up. Other than that, it looks as good as new." Both the mechanic and Rusty laughed.

"I think this here can of lubricant in your crank case might loosen up that rod until you get home and can take off the head. We'll put some oil in her, put in a new gas filter, tighten up this belt, and you should be ready to go."

"While I'm here, we might as well top off the diesel fuel."

"That will be seventy two dollars and fifty cents," said the mechanic.

Rusty dug around in his pocket, came up with the seventy dollars, and had to search through the litter in his ute to find another two dollars and fifty cents.

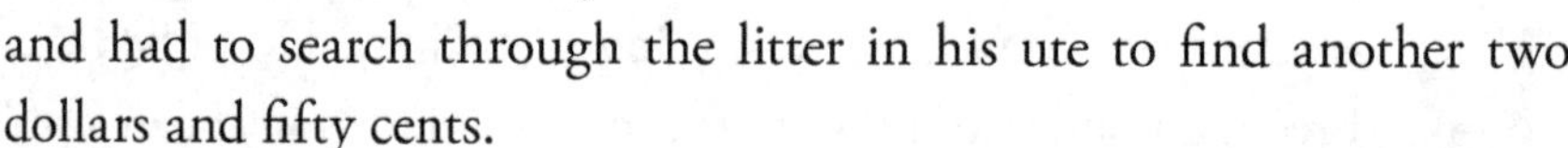

One could not make the whole drive from Lightning Ridge to Sydney in one day, so Rusty drove as far as Katoomba and again stayed at the Traveler's Rest motel.

* * *

The next day, Rusty was up early, ate at the Boomerang Café, and was in Sydney and down at The Rocks by 10:00 A.M. He didn't want to spend money for the parking ramp, so he drove around the side streets where he found a place he could legally park and not be bothered with someone wanting to tow his ute. He ended up about ten blocks from where he wanted to be, which was down at the wharf where he and Kate had been before on George Street.

On the side streets in the area were several cheap hotels. Rusty knew this area, since years earlier, he had worked in Sydney, in addition coming here to see his ex-wife. He found one of the hotels he had previously stayed in called the Ritz; however, it was anything but ritzy. He signed up for a small single bedroom on the fourth floor. Nothing fancy. It looked almost like a prison cell. However, Rusty was only looking for some place to sleep.

By 11:00 A.M., Rusty was walking down George Street. He didn't look like anyone from Sydney. While his clothes were clean, his dark brown, long sleeve shirt had seen better days and had a couple of tears in it. His blue jeans were also well-worn and had a couple of tears. His boots were dirty, as was his rather disheveled Akubra hat. One could definitely tell he had recently came out of the Australian bush. He turned down Argyle Street and then right down Kendall Lane. There he found a small jewelry store with the address of the two Serbs who had purchased the big diamond at the opal festival for fifty thousand dollars.

Entering the jewelry store, Rusty spotted Drago Vujic, the Serb Rusty had spoken to in Lightning Ridge, sitting behind the counter.

"Hi, Drago. You remember me?" said Rusty.

With a Serbian accent, Drago responded, "Yes. Rusty, isn't it?"

"That's right. You said you might have an interest in some diamonds."

"What did you bring me?" said Drago.

Rusty pulled out from his pocket all three of the diamonds he brought with him from Lightning Ridge.

Drago, expressionless, laid out a fine jeweler's cloth, picked up his jeweler's eyepiece, and examined all three diamonds. The stones were beautiful. The largest stone weighed 5 carats and the other two were 2.1 and 2.3 in carat weight. They were exceptional stones.

Rusty, rather than telling Drago what he wanted for the three stones, instead asked Drago what he would pay. A big mistake on Rusty's part. Rusty's appearance and demeanor gave Drago the impression that Rusty didn't know what he had and that maybe Rusty wasn't that bright.

"I'll give you two hundred dollars each for the two, 2 carat stones and five hundred dollars for the larger stone." Rusty, shocked, didn't know what to say. Had he been negotiating the sale of opals, Rusty would have known how to respond, but instead, he glanced around the jewelry store, feigning interest in the rings, necklaces, and watches that crowded the pristinely polished display counters. He rubbed his chin between his thumb and pointer finger, pretending to weigh his options, but really just remembering what Kate and he had gotten for the two stones they sold in Sydney five years earlier and also the two, 2 carat stones the Russian from Melbourne had paid at the Opal Festival.

Recalling how Kate would negotiate, he attempted to play it cool and reject the offer.

"Too low," Rusty finally responded, his voice slightly shaky. "I think I'll go somewhere else." But instead of plucking his diamonds from the jeweler's cloth and immediately pulling away from the counter, he hesitated, and dropped his hands to his sides.

He and Drago both focused on the dewy glaze Rusty's hands had left upon the otherwise immaculately polished counter.

Drago, without removing his jeweler's eyepiece, closely eyed Rusty, who still had not moved. Drago smiled slyly. He had no trouble reading Rusty. He had been reading people his whole life. He was an expert on knowing who to push and how far to push them. It was his turn to feign interest in the jewelry store's familiar interior.

"I'll tell you what," Drago said, "you change your mind, you know where to find me. I change my mind, I know where to find you."

Standing across from Drago with only the counter between them, Rusty suddenly felt very vulnerable. Knowing that he had been beat, he nodded slightly, plucked the three diamonds from the jeweler's cloth, turned on his heels, and walked stiffly out of the store in a daze, unsure what to do next.

* * *

Rusty had arrived in Sydney with high hopes: Sell some diamonds for a wad of cash, then head back to Lightning Ridge in a new ute and take Sue out on the town, maybe in a new suit of clothes. Maybe give Sue some money for a new outfit. Or was that too much? Too pushy? Maybe take her out to buy some clothes. Not Lighting Ridge clothes, though.

They could go to Sydney. Stay at a nice hotel. Walk in the park. Maybe this park. Rusty looked around. Which park was this?

He turned in place a couple of times, the lowering sun causing him to squint as he spun, trying to figure out where he was. He remembered wandering south down Kendall and hanging a right at Argyle, but had he turned left or right after that? As he turned, looking for clues, he thought he recognized someone he knew across the park, a dusty, broken man, sporting a splintered wooden crutch, with hand outstretched toward a young couple being walked by a bitzer.

The man glanced over at him, and Rusty averted his eyes, not wanting the man to think he was staring him down or, worse yet, offering a handout. By the time he looked back up, the man was hobbling into a small grove of trees, followed closely by a couple of Blue Heelers on dero patrol. Rusty rubbed his eyes. Shook his head at himself. *Who would I know in Sydney?* he thought. *I need half a slab. Or a full slab and a drunk. Or at least a boozer and a half a drunk. But where?* He was sure he had passed one as he wondered into this park of happy people holding hands, tossing Frisbee, and picnicking. But where had he entered the park? To get his bearings, he found the sun and turned himself West, knowing that the wharfs of Circular Quay lay somewhere East of Kendall.

"Can I help you?"

He jerked, startled by the woman who had appeared, seemingly out of thin air, before him.

Rusty stammered, "Um. Huh. Um."

"Sorry." She extended her hand. "Milla. Not short for Camilla."

To his right, someone shouted, "Look out, dipstick!" He turned to see a lanky rollerblader speeding toward him. To avoid a certain collision, Rusty stepped toward Milla, causing her to step back and causing the top heel of her red, almond toe pump to slide neatly into a crack in the sidewalk. As she stumbled backward, Rusty grasped her still outstretched hand and steadied her.

"Nice save," Milla said.

With his free hand, Rusty touched the brim of his hat, and for a moment, the two stood awkwardly holding hands in what appeared to be a frozen handshake.

Rusty was the first to let go. "Rusty."

"You don't seem too rusty to me." Milla smoothed her dress and worked her foot, attempting to remove her shoe from the concrete teeth of the sidewalk.

"No. That's my name," Rusty said.

"Sorry," she said, not looking up from her shoe. "You didn't name me," he said.

Milla laughed.

Rusty smiled. "Can I help you with that," he said, pointing to her shoe, which was still stuck in the sidewalk. "Yes, please." Milla gingerly slid her foot from her pump as Rusty knelt to the sidewalk. He quickly worked his finger into the crack in the sidewalk and pushed up on the top lift. He slid her pump to her, and she inserted it just as gingerly as she had removed it. "This must be how Cinderella felt." Rusty laughed and stood up. "You look like Cinderella, but I'm one dag of a Prince Charming."

Milla smiled. "You seem lost. What are you looking for?" "A cheap boozer, first of all." He looked her over, decided she wasn't likely to rob him, and said, "And to maybe sell a few diamonds to pay for some beer."

"You're in luck. I know a cheap boozer." She leaned in close enough for a wisp of her golden hair to brush against his cheek and whispered as if the world were listening, "And I know a diamond buyer."

"Ace! Just tell me where and who, Cinderella." "You know The Lord Nelson?"

"Never heard of him."

Milla laughed. "That's the boozer."

Rusty smiled. He felt his face redden, and he hoped Milla couldn't see the shade change beneath the shadow of his Akubra hat.

"We'll meet there, and I'll introduce you to the buyer." Milla jotted the name of the pub down on a slip of paper she had pulled from a small handbag. She handed it to Rusty and smiled. "In case you forget."

After his embarrassment, he doubted he would forget, but he took the paper anyway, glanced at it, and stuffed it into his shirt pocket. "How far is it?"

"Turn back the way you came—"

Rusty interrupted, "How do you know which way I came?"

Milla laughed nervously, embarrassed. "I saw you head down here from George Street. You looked lost."

"And you stalked me." Rusty smiled. "I've been stalked by more dangerous women than you, Cinderella, so I'll let this one slide."

"Thank you for your pardon, my lord," Milla said, mimicking a curtsy.

"So how do I get there from George Street?" "Head north until you see Argyle—"

"Was just there."

"Are you going to let me finish?" Milla smiled. "Pardon, my lady."

"Hang a left at Argyle and walk five minutes. It will be on your right. A big stone building."

"And you thought I would forget that quickly?"

"It was a joke. A bad one. Obviously." She felt her face redden, but she wore no Akubra hat to hide it.

Rusty was suddenly embarrassed for her. "No worries." He glanced around. "Want to walk with me?"

"I have a couple things to do." She thumbed over her shoulder. "A few things at the office. I'll meet you there in ten or fifteen."

Rusty nodded, touched the brim of his hat. "In ten or fifteen, Cinderella." With a smile, he brushed past Milla close enough to smell the floral scent of her hair. Two minutes later, he was walking up the sandstone steps that lead to George Street on his way to get a pint or two and try his hand at another diamond deal.

* * *

Rusty walked into The Lord Nelson and looked the place over. A large L-shaped bar sat in the corner; a half-dozen chalkboards advertising recent brews hung end-to-end like cheap jewels in a jester's crown. Two dozen wooden tables littered the room, as if someone had neglected to clean up after an all-night rage. The pub had seen better days, but by Rusty's accounts, the pub still had a lot of days left in it. All of it was fancier than Rusty would have liked, but it was about as much a boozer as you could expect in the big city. As he approached the bar, the tender raised his eyebrow.

"Gimme a handle of whatever brew is on that chalkboard over my head," Rusty said.

At the end of the bar, a man raised his head, mumbled, and dropped his head hard onto the faux-gold elbow bar attached to the counter.

"Better gimme two," Rusty said. "I have some catching up to do."

The bartend filled two mugs, slid them across the counter to Rusty, and approached the mumbling man.

"Nice bloke," Rusty mumbled to himself. He took his two pints to a table in the corner and sat facing the door.

Fifteen minutes later, he took his two empty mugs to the bartender. "Gimme another." He returned to his table and slowly sipped his amber fluid, hoping to give Milla the impression that he had not been here long.

An empty glass and thirty minutes later, Rusty called out to the bartender. "Gimme another and some fish and chips."

The bartender filled Rusty another mug and brought it to him. Rusty eyed him suspiciously. "You put in my order of fish and chips?"

The bartender nodded and turned back toward the counter.

"Hey, bartender," Rusty said, "cat got your tongue?"

The bartender turned to Rusty and opened his mouth wide, revealing a dark, empty hole.

"Fair suck of the sav." Rusty touched the brim of his hat. "Sorry, bloke."

The bartender returned 10 minutes later and dropped the plate of fish and chips in front of Rusty.

Rusty pointed to his empty mug. "How about another?" When the bartender returned carrying two full mugs, Rusty nodded. He felt the two of them had an understanding.

"Listen, bloke, a woman ever stand you up even though you had a fistful of diamonds to give her?"

The bartender patted Rusty on the shoulder and returned to the counter.

Two hours and a half dozen mugs later, Milla sashayed through the open door.

"Cinderella," Rusty slurred. "Somebody has the wobbly boot on."

"What'd you expect sending a thirsty Australian Outbacker to a bar?" Rusty dug deep into his pants pocket, pulled out the diamonds, and dropped them on the table. "Name your price, Cinderella."

Milla quickly cupped the diamonds under her hand and looked around. "Rusty, you don't know the kinds of people around here." She quickly plucked the diamonds one by one from the table, scarred with the initials of patrons long gone. She peered at the diamonds, sparkling up at her from the palm of her hand. "These are fine specimens."

"How would you know? You the buyer or something?" "I am." She extended her hand. "Milla the buyer. Nice to meet you."

Rusty sloppily shook her hand. "I shoulda known." "How much do you want for the lot?" "I'm a man of my word, Cinderella. You name the price." "I honestly wouldn't know. I'm new to the diamond business. I usually deal in rubies, opals, some gold—" "Opals?" Rusty drained another pint. "I know opals.

Diamonds now that's—"

"Did I say opals?" Milla laughed, feigning embarrassment. "I meant pearls. People always pawning pearls." She laughed. "I'm almost a poet."

"Almost." Rusty turned toward the counter. "Bartender. How about another?" He turned toward Milla. "Anything for you?"

"Nothing." Milla closed her hand around diamonds, protecting them from the drunk and wandering eyes of a raucous mob of men who had just stumbled through the front door.

Paying no attention to the men, the bartender brought another pint to Rusty.

"Nice bloke," Rusty said. "Never shuts up." Rusty studied Milla studying the diamonds. The ends of her hair hung like a fragile golden frame around the delicate curve of her face. She certainly was pretty, not the kind of Lightning Ridge pretty that Rusty preferred, but a cosmopolitan pretty that Rusty found difficult to define. "Give me a thousand for the lot."

Milla looked up. "You really are a dag." "Nine hundred?"

"Not a chance."

"I can't go any lower."

"Good. That's too low already."

"But I don't have any docs to back up where these came from."

She studied him carefully.

"You don't know about the Kimberley process?" "I'm aware, but I just don't care."

"You really are a poet. That you don't care is music to my ears."

She smiled. "That's good, but I can't take them off your hands for the price you named."

Rusty downed the last drops of his beer. "I shoulda known."

"How about two thousand?"

"Fair dinkum!" Rusty slammed his mug onto the table. "It's a deal." Rusty smiled ear-to-ear as Milla stuffed the diamonds into her tiny purse and dug around for payment. A moment later, Milla slid twenty neatly and tightly folded $100 dollar bills across the table to Rusty, all the while keeping the tiny stack of cash hidden beneath her slightly cupped hand.

Rusty took the money from beneath her palm and fanned it in front of his face, paying no attention to who could be paying attention. "Fair dinkum!" he again called out.

Milla glanced around, opened her mouth to speak, then closed it again.

"I'll tell you what," Rusty said, tucking the now crumpled bills into his pants pocket, "you are a mysterious woman Milla…Milla…." Rusty lifted his hat slightly and scratched his head. "You never told me your last name."

"You never told me yours."

Rusty thought for a moment and finally decided he didn't want Milla to know too much about him. "Fair enough," he said.

"Fair enough," she said, rising from the table. She extended her hand. "Nice doing business with you, Rusty."

Rusty shook her hand. "The same," he said.

She held his hand a little longer than necessary, then let it go. "I'll be seeing you."

As Rusty watch Milla waltz out the door as smoothly as she had sashayed in, he knew this trip to Sydney was over, and he was glad to be heading back to Lightning Ridge tomorrow.

CHAPTER 5

BRUCE'S LUCKY DAY

The events in this chapter are happening in parallel to the previous chapter.

* * *

T*his must be my lucky day*, Bruce thought as he thumbed through the wad of bills he had collected from the drangos milling about the parks and wharfs.

Despite the hoard of money Bruce had stolen over five years ago from the whackers in Lightning Ridge and his two former partners, may the Devil have their souls, he had none of the moolah remaining, having spent it on women, wine, weapons, and women, and more women, and a little more wine in between the women. He smiled to himself.

No regrets. None except for this bum leg and that I never got mine from that ratbag Rusty and dog Kate.

Bruce wadded the bills into his fist and stuffed the cash into his pants pocket in time to see a cute couple meandering his way, walking a mangy bitzer. *This one should be easy*, he thought. *A root rat looking for a naughty always spreads the cash around when he's with a little spunk.*

He hobbled toward them with his shoddy wooden crutch that he used more as an actor's prop than an actual prop. "How 'bout helping a poor wharfie get a meal or a cool drink on this hot Australian day?" For effect, he glanced up at the sky. From the corner of his eye, he saw a man turning slowly in place. While the boy dug in his pocket for a handout, Bruce zeroed in on his next score, who was obviously lost, obviously a tourist, and obviously an easy score.

But who the turning man was surprised him. "Well, take a squizz at this," Bruce said to himself, as he watched the man. "If it's not that ratbag Rusty."

As if he had heard his name called out, Rusty looked in Bruce's direction, held his gaze for a moment, and then looked away. "Wuss," Bruce mumbled.

Stepping back into character, Bruce held out his hand,

"How about that piece of meal for this tired wharfie?"

The young man dropped a handful of coins, a piece of bubble gum, and a plastic button into Bruce's hand. "God be with you," the man said.

Across the common area, Bruce spotted two jacks easing their way toward him. "God's done forgot about me," Bruce said, as he hobbled toward a stand of trees and a thicket of bushes huddled against the south side of the Museum of Contemporary Art. *I'm glad He has forgot, 'cause now all the luck I make is my own.*

* * *

From the tangle of bushes that Bruce called home, he watched the jacks amble away toward the mobile lemonade stand rolling West toward George Street. Halfway across the park, he spotted Rusty, who was now talking to a tall, thin, wide-shouldered blonde. Bruce watched as Rusty brushed past the woman, smiling, and strode toward George Street, as if he owned the whole town. The woman remained standing where Rusty had left her until Rusty had turned North onto George Street. She then followed Rusty's path through the park and onto George Street, keeping a short distance between herself and Rusty, as if she did not want Rusty to see her. Bruce scrambled through the shrubs to the retaining wall that separated the Museum of Contemporary Art from George Street and waited until both Rusty and the woman were far enough down George Street that they wouldn't notice that a dirty old man seemed to be following them.

At Argyle, both Rusty and the woman turned west. However, shortly thereafter, the woman turned North onto Kendall Lane, as Rusty continued to head West on Argyle. *I'll get my hands on that Mappa Tassie another day,* Bruce thought, as he zeroed in on Rusty weaving his way through a throng of people. *Today, I'm taking care of at least one of those loose ends from Lightning Ridge.*

* * *

A couple of minutes later, Bruce watched Rusty enter The Lord Nelson. *Ah, The Lord Nelson, it's been a while,* Bruce thought, as he studied the concrete block façade of Sydney's oldest hotel. Across the street from The Lord Nelson and in front of a recently abandoned storefront, Bruce spotted a long roll-off dumpster behind which he could hide and still see foot traffic coming from the both the West and East of the bar.

As he propped himself against a telephone pole, a voice behind him called out, "How 'bout a little something for an old wharfie?" Bruce squinted into the darkness of the deep entryway that led into the abandoned store, and he immediately recognized Ol' One Eye, although he had seen him only once over two years ago.

By that time ***two years ago****, Bruce had already burned through all of the money he had stolen in Lightning Ridge, but he had recently won the right from Ugly Joe to bum the wharfs of Circular Quay when he had made Ugly Joe an offer he couldn't refuse.*

"Ugly Joe, huh?" Bruce said, startling the man who was sound asleep on a park bench in First Fleet Park.

Ugly Joe squinted up at him. "Who you?" "A friend."

Ugly Joe sat up, and Bruce sat down beside him. "How'd you get that name?"

Ugly Joe opened his worn jacket, pulled a tattered photograph of a handsome young bloke from his pocket, and handed it to Bruce. "I used to be a model, a magazine model." He gazed out at the docked ferries, filling with people. "One night, I fell asleep behind the wheel of my auto, smashed into a diesel rig, and about burnt up. They said my face was like melted wax when they pulled me out."

Bruce looked up from the photo and into Ugly Joe's eyes. "You are an ugly dero, but how would you like to be uglier?" Bruce tore the photo in half, turned it, tore it in half again, and tossed the pieces into the ocean breeze.

Ugly Joe leaped up. "Hey now—"

Without breaking his stern gaze into Ugly Joe's eyes, Bruce leaned forward and tapped the hilt of the dagger peeking over the top of his boot. "Listen, friend, there's not enough handouts to go around. I'm giving you an opportunity to change your career path on your own…before I do it for you."

Ugly Joe stood for a moment, holding Bruce's gaze, before turning and walking away.

The last time Bruce saw him, it was a warm summer night on the wharfs of Circular Quay, and Ugly Joe was pinned between a wharf and an empty ferry, the ebb and flow of the black tide squeezing screams from his bloody mouth. "Let me help, friend," Bruce said, lowing his battered wooden crutch into Ugly Joe's face. He worked the crutch into his broken mouth and held him below water until he struggled no more.

* * *

A week later, Bruce pulled himself from the tangle of shrubs he had made into his home only to find Ol' One Eye with his arthritis-gnarled hand outstretched to people in the park.

Bruce approached him and said nothing.

Ol' One Eye looked him over. "A dollar for an old wharfie?" "This territory is mine."

"By whose accounts?" "By mine and Emil's."

Ol' One Eye looked him over. "I'm blind in one eye, and I can't well see out of the other, but I don't see no Emil."

Bruce tapped his boot with his crutch. "Emil's my mate with a razor sharp seven inch donger, who'll root any bloke who stands in my way."

Without saying a word, Ol' One Eye turned and exited First Fleet Park and had never entered the park again. However, over the years, Bruce had heard that the old man had been hooking his fish upstream, but Bruce had been unable to catch him and any time away from the park was time he was not making money.

Now to find Ol' One Eye here while Bruce was pursuing other business was a lucky break. "My lucky day," Bruce muttered to himself, as he turned his attention back to The Lord Nelson. Although he was not the man he once was, he knew he would be finished with this before Rusty had taken his first draught.

He slowly pulled Emil from his worn Outbacker's boot and wedged the end of the tip of the dagger into the telephone pole behind him. Grasping the hilt, he pulled himself up, removed the dagger from the pole, and held it close to his body. He checked East and West on the sidewalks of Argyle. No pedestrians. And the roll-off blocked the entryway from the road traffic, so no worries there. He turned his gaze back to The Lord Nelson and eased backward into the darkness of the recessed entryway.

"I got something for you, Ol' One Eye," he said, as he quickly leaned forward and covered the dero's mouth. "You remember Emil?" Without waiting for even a nod, Bruce swiftly and smoothly sliced the dagger across Ol' One Eye's weathered throat. "That'll learn you to poach in another man's territory."

Bruce wiped the bloody blade against Ol' One Eye's tattered jacket. In an attempt to absorb some of the blood gushing from the man's throat, Bruce pulled the collar tight. From the store window, he removed a faded cardboard sign and placed it between the bleeding man and the open sidewalk, hoping to absorb the blood before it trickled from the darkness into the light. He glanced up at the sky and noted that the sun had passed the point where it would illuminate this entryway, so there was no way anyone would see Ol' One Eye until tomorrow, unless they were walking into the abandoned store.

Satisfied with his job, he moved back into the light and propped himself against the telephone pole. *Been two years since I killed a man, and it felt so good that, today, I'm going to make it two.*

* * *

While waiting for some action at The Lord Nelson, Bruce rose and stretched several times, picked the pockets of the newly deceased Ol' One Eye, watched the girls walk by, and, finally, whistled to himself when he witnessed the woman he had seen with Rusty walking up the street toward The Lord Nelson almost two hours later.

"I'll be a tinny kangaroo," Bruce muttered to himself.

She fluffed her hair and plastered on a smile before sashaying through the door and taking a sharp right. Bruce pulled himself up, picked up his crutch, and jaywalked across the street.

He pulled up close to the building and craned his neck to peer through the window at the booth where Rusty and the woman sat. "What kind of business would Rusty have with such a little spunk?"

As if hearing his question and obligingly answering, Rusty dropped three beautiful diamonds on the table. The woman scooped them up, looked around. Bruce quickly pulled his head back and stood, speechless, thoughtless, and dumbfounded by his increasingly good luck.

Finally, the noise of a crowd of raucous men pulled him out of his temporary stupor as they entered the bar.

"How 'bout a pitcher for each of us, Felix?"

Bruce again peered inside. This time searching out and finding the bartender. He laughed quietly to himself. *I'm surprised he's still alive after the cut I gave that cat.*

Felix slid around the corner of the bar much the way he had the first time (and the last time) Bruce saw him.

"Gimme a lager," Bruce had demanded of Felix **several years** *ago. "Something strong. What it cost don't matter."*

Felix leaned across the counter close to Bruce and said quietly, "Owner of this place bought a bottle of Snake Venom at auction, but it'll cost you."

Mimicking the bartender's attempt at confidentiality, Bruce leaned forward, shortening the distance between him and Felix, but instead of whispering, he shouted: "What it cost don't matter!" Felix jumped back, nearly clearing the counter as he did. A woman in the corner, clearly a tourist from the States said, "Oh, my," and left the bar. Bruce turned to the remaining half-dozen, now staring, patrons. "You best go somewhere else if you don't like to see a man drink to get drunk."

A group of office folk tossed a few dollars on their table and left. The only patron remaining raised his glass in a toast to Bruce, downed his pint, and asked the bartender for another.

Felix moved to pour the man another drink, but Bruce stopped him by throwing a bowl of stale snack mix across the bar. To Felix he said, "That one's mine." He glared at the patron. "They all mine."

The man rose and left the bar, shooting a concerned look at Felix.

"Nothing to be concerned about here," Bruce said to the man.

He turned to Felix. "Now where's that Venom?"

Felix bent to access a compartment behind the counter. "What you got there?" Bruce asked, leaning across the counter to watch Felix.

"Owner keeps this in a safe," Felix said, turning the wheel to the combination. "Said not to sell it for less than two hundred dollars a bottle."

"Two hundred dollars a bottle? I've had water cost more 'n' that."

"What kind of water was that?" Felix held tight to the Snake Venom.

"Outback water. You in the Outback with no water and someone has water, you pay whatever you got to get it. Now how 'bout that venom?"

"Pay first for this one." "Don't trust me?"

"I trust you fine. It's your thirst I don't trust."

Bruce laughed and tossed four hundred dollars on the counter. "Gimme another."

"This is all we have. Probably only one left in Sydney." Bruce glared at the bartender.

"It's all you'll need," Felix said, plucking two one hundred dollar bills off the stack and setting the bottle on the counter.

"I'll be the judge."

Bruce picked it up to drink, but in the excitement, Felix had not removed the lid. The metal cap cracked against Bruce's front teeth. Without missing a beat, Bruce pinched the lid between his molars and used them as a bottle opener. He spit the lid in Felix's surprised face before downing the venom in a single draught.

Ten minutes later, Bruce was face down on the counter. Twenty minutes later, he was hobbling around The Lord Nelson, attempting to dance, and talking gibberish about some old friends and a mine shaft. Thirty minutes later, he was back at his seat at the counter. "How 'bout another of those?"

Felix opened his mouth to respond, then stopped. He bent below the counter, fiddled with the safe, and pretended to pull a non-existent bottle of Snake Venom from under the counter, grabbing, instead a bottle of XXXX. "Two hundred."

Bruce tossed two one hundred dollar bills on the counter. As Felix reached to scoop them from the table, Bruce grabbed his wrist. Bruce studied Felix. "How much you hear?"

Felix shook his head. "I don't know what—"

"'Bout them dead guys," Bruce said as he began to pull Felix across the counter. Felix fought, but Bruce, despite his hard fall down a mineshaft less than a month ago, was amazingly strong, and when he had pulled Felix far enough across the counter to grab his other arm, it took only a moment to drag him the rest of the way across the counter. Bruce tossed the man to the floor, placed the foot of his bad leg against Felix's throat, and awkwardly dragged him behind the counter.

Once behind the counter, Bruce removed his foot from Felix's throat and dropped beside the man, immediately forcing his elbow onto Felix's throat. With his free hand, Bruce reached down to his boot and pulled out his dagger. "Emil'll make sure you don't tell nobody nothing."

Felix fought, but the weight of Bruce's elbow against his throat kept him from both screaming and taking in air, weakening him. With the tip of his dagger, Bruce pried open Felix's mouth, the razor sharp edges of the dagger slicing the sides of Felix's mouth as he fought. In one quick motion, Bruce lifted his elbow from Felix's throat, and as the injured man opened his mouth to gasp for air, Bruce pulled his tongue tight and sliced it through with his dagger.

Bruce smiled as the severed tongue slithered in his hand like the detached head of a bloody snake. He quickly rose, grabbed his crutch, and, when heading to the door, dropped the tongue on the table where Rusty and the woman now sat.

Good times, Bruce **now** thought as he stood outside The Lord Nelson, his back against the cinderblock wall.

He peered in the window in time to see Rusty fan several hundred dollar bills in front of his face. Knowing that the transaction was finished, Bruce watched for a little longer than he had before to make sure that no one was escaping from an unknown exit. It didn't take long for him to see the woman rise from the table, take Rusty's hand, and walk toward the door, toward Bruce.

Two years since I killed a man. Two weeks since I touched a woman without paying first. There's no sense in living like a saint, Bruce thought, as he clasped the woman's wrist, covered her mouth, and pulled her into a tiny alley that had no exit except through him.

Bruce tossed her on the ground and placed the foot of his bad leg against her throat. *The more things change,* he thought, as he removed his foot from her throat and dropped quickly beside her.

"What you got there in your pretty little purse?"

He pulled Emil from his boot and sliced open the bag. Three diamonds fell onto the ground along with a stack of one hundred dollar bills and a Beretta Pico.

"Aren't you full of surpr—"

From behind him, a man asked calmly in a heavy Serbian accent, "What you doing there, swagman?"

Without turning, Bruce said, "None of your business, friend."

Another man, also with a heavy Serbian accent said,

"But I think it is. It is isn't it, Alek?"

"It is, Mirko. But the name's Aleksandar."

Bruce, plucking the three diamonds from the ground, said, "Take your spat elsewhere, Alek." "Not without the woman," Alek said.

"Find your own," Bruce said, finally turning, but without allowing the woman to rise.

The shock on Bruce's face caused the larger of the two very large men to laugh. "Didn't expect such a handsome man, did he, Mirko?"

Mirko stepped forward, just behind Alek. "Doesn't look like he did. Now hand over the woman."

Bruce quickly pulled Emil and lunged at the Alek's legs. Alek sidestepped, but not quickly enough, and Emil pierced deep into his calve. But instead of howling in pain, he laughed and dropped hard onto Bruce's back, his elbow striking him in the spine.

Bruce tried to roll, but Alek's weight kept him from moving.

Mirko stepped forward, and wrapped two large hands around Bruce's throat.

Bruce tried to bite, to lunge, to kick, but now the woman had his legs.

"Nice move, Milla," Mirko said.

The last words he heard before he passed out were from

Milla, "Tonight, we'll take this one down to the wharf."

* * *

Darkness.

Bruce blinked his eyes. Held them open wide.

Slowly, his eyes began to distinguish a thin seam of light to his left. He looked up. Darkness. Back to the left. Seam of light.

He tried to laugh to himself, but the pain in the back of his head was too severe to do anything except blink.

A lifetime ago was the last time I saw the inside of a trunk, *he thought*. Five years old. Or was I six? My mum's boyfriend. Gary? Harry? *A thin seam of light. Three gunshots, then three circular rays of light through the trunk lid.*

Was he trying to kill me? How close had he come? T*he smell of gasoline. A dead baby gator to his right, staring back at him.* Was this then or now, *he thought*?

That was then.

Eventually, they found me. How many days was I there? Long enough for the gator to begin to smell. Not long enough to start eating the gator. Found me in a parking lot. Unharmed.

That was then. This is **now**.

They won't find me unharmed this time. Will they even find me? If I don't come out fighting, they'll never have a chance to find me.

He moved his arms, his legs. Both bound. He would have to bite. He clenched his jaws, ground his teeth. Shattered. He remembered something about that. Something about the business end of a cricket bat. He moved his head. His neck was sore, but he could still use it.

He closed his eyes, relaxed himself to sleeping until the trunk opened an untold number of hours later.

Lights in his face. Darkness elsewhere. Alek and Mirko speaking a language he didn't understand. Behind them, Milla said, "Make it fast. Drago has places to go."

Alek grabbed him under the arms, and Mirko grabbed his legs. They lifted together and pulled him from the car. He lay limp until Milla leaned close over him. When she got close enough for him to smell the floral scent of her hair, he bucked hard.

His forehead struck her square in the mouth, sending her reeling backwards. The men dropped him to the ground, and a moment later, Milla screamed and splashed into the water.

He rolled to his right onto his back under the car and raised his arms to a rusty fold of steel protruding from the car's undercarriage.

He pushed and sawed hard. The plastic tie quickly snapped. He rolled onto his stomach, swung his legs further beneath the car, and peered out into the darkness, searching for some sign of where the men might be.

Finally, he made out the faint silhouette of Alek crouching at the edge of the wharf, his back toward Bruce. Mirko, he assumed, was finding a flashlight. Bruce knew he had only seconds.

Do I lunge at Alek? Wait for some sign of Mirko? Have I ever waited for anything?

He bent his legs and tucked the feet of his still-bound legs into the car's undercarriage. He grasped the underside of the rear bumper with his arms and with one smooth movement rocketed himself from beneath the car toward Alek.

The man tumbled into the water on top of the woman. Bruce rose as quickly as he could, his legs still bound and his bad leg paining him more after the exertion of propelling him from beneath the car. He turned in time to see Mirko running toward him with a floodlight.

Bruce dropped to the ground, and Mirko tumbled over him to the water. Bruce stood, and without turning to look at the two men and the woman struggling in the water, he hopped his way to the still-running car and dropped into the driver's seat.

He instantly heard the unnerving click and felt the hard nose of a gun against the back of his head. He glanced into the rearview mirror. A man who looked as if he belonged behind a jewelry counter much more than he belonged behind a loaded Taurus 1911 peered back at him. In a heavy Serbian accent, the man told Bruce to get out of the car.

Bruce slowly opened the door and pulled himself from the car. Alek, Mirko, and Milla, were there to meet him. Bruce, always one to see the darkest of humor in every situation, raised his arms and smiled. "Be my guest," he said.

"We'll make sure we finish him off this time," Milla said, peering into the backseat of the car at the man still pointing the gun at Bruce.

Without smiling, Alek and Mirko lifted him from beneath each of his outstretched arms. While they lifted him and turned him toward the water, Bruce inquired of Milla, "What kind of lipstick is that, beauty? Bloody red?"

The men tossed him into the water. Instantly, Bruce dove into the darkness. Gunshots reverberated through the water, and bullets traced around him. Mirko flipped on a floodlight and a beam of light followed him down.

He dove as deep as he could and turned to look up. A bullet struck him in the shoulder; another struck his chest. Instinct took over, and he fought to resurface. Another bullet in his chest pushed him further into the darkness, and as he began to descend, he peered up into the floodlight. The seaweed on the surface broke the floodlight's beam into a dozen pieces, and the edges of the floodlight's beam were broken into a thousand points of light by the rippling water.

Looks like diamonds raining down on me, he thought, as he descended past the point of return into the darkness of Sydney Cove. *Must be my lucky day.*

CHAPTER 6

EMILIJA NOVAK

The events in this chapter are happening in parallel to the previous two chapters.

* * *

"Emilija," Drago called out, shortly after the door leading from the jewelry store closed behind Rusty. "I have another one for you. This one probably bigger than the last."

In the office up the stairs behind Drago, Milla raised the blinds that shuttered the windows that looked down on Kendall Lane. She saw Rusty with head down, walking, almost wandering, East down Kendall. She grabbed a tiny handbag from her desk and raced down the stairs.

"Why did you let him out so fast, Drago?"

"To make you worth your commission," Drago replied, not looking up from the jewelry counter he was polishing.

She made her way to a jewelry counter on the other side of the store, reached beneath the counter, pulled from it a Beretta Pico, and stuffed the gun in her purse. "You know I'm worth more than my commission," she said.

"And you make that on your side businesses, whatever those might be."

She eyed him. "You know what they are. You get more than your share of those commissions, too, Drago."

He mumbled under his breath, shined the counters with his jeweler's cloth.

"What was that, Drago?"

"You'd better get on his trail, Emilija."

"He's not going to be hard to find," she said, leaning into a mirror to check her hair. "And call me Milla."

"I'll call you what I please when you're working for me," he said, handing her the piece of paper on which he had written Rusty's name.

"And when you're working for me…" Milla paused and stared hard at Drago, causing him to look up from the jewelry case. "You won't last long."

* * *

Milla stepped onto Kendall in time to see Rusty turn left onto Argyle. She wondered where he was heading, if he knew where he was going, if he knew where he came from, really knew where he came from. She thought of herself, where she came from, where she was heading. She knew those things now, but she did not always know those things.

***Long ago**, when she was a girl of nine years old, she knew where she was going. She knew that she would always be like a little girl, living close to her father, mother, three older brothers, and baby sister, Mira. Even at that young age, she had chosen the house where she would live—a narrow two story house only three houses down from her parent's tiny house in the happy village of Bosanski Brod. Her brothers would likely live across town, being independent of their parents, in the way that boys are. Her baby sister would live with their parents until she was grown and would inherit the* *family home when her parents were gone, which young Emilija knew would be many, many years away.*

But then there was the war. Her brothers enlisted immediately, soldiered to the front lines during that brief period when there was still a chance of victory. The front lines quickly collapsed and most of the young foot-soldiers were mown down with it. Her father enlisted when the inventory of young men had been depleted and her mother even took up arms when the front line became a jagged front of fighting scattered among the ruins of their once beautiful village.

The fighting quickly swept through the village, transitioning from the tiny streets into the tiny homes, the living rooms, the bedrooms, the closets, and finally tearing open the hiding places between the walls and floors that were reserved for only the smallest of the small villagers.

Milla remembers sitting huddled between the walls of her parent's home and their neighbor's home, staring into the darkness, her sister tucked like a chick beneath young Emilija's arm. Outside the wall, the shouts of the men and the screams of the women were not mixed with those of her father and mother she told herself.

"No, those are not mamma and poppa," she whispered to her sister.

"It is," Mira whispered. "I heard her call my name."

"That is another Mira," Emilija lied. "Now hush before they hear us."

But it was too late.

Outside the wall there was a large crash, as the pantry that concealed the false wall panel fell to the floor. The panel was quickly pulled back. First, several guns poked into the space, like alien eyes searching for life. Then there were arms, reaching into the darkness. They grabbed Emilija violently by the shoulders and tossed her onto the broken china that lay scattered across the kitchen floor. A moment later, Mira landed beside her, screaming in pain and fear. Emilija reached out to comfort her, but before her fingers could brush the hair from her sister's

face, Emilija was lifted from the floor and tossed over the shoulder of a Republican soldier.

"This will make a good one," the soldier said to another beside him. "Young, but not too young."

Emilija called out to her sister, "Run!" But she only lay there, screaming, as Emilija was carried out the door.

* * *

Now Milla pulled herself out of her memories. Her face was wet and her expression had hardened. She dabbed at her eyes and tried to soften her features.

"Turn that frown upside down, the Americans say," she said to herself. "No worries, the Australians say."

She took a deep breath. A half block in front of her, Rusty ambled into First Fleet Park. She picked up her pace so as not to lose track of him. When she spotted him in the middle of the park, she smiled and thought, *Little chance of that happening.* She watched as he turned slowly in place, obviously just realizing that he did not know where he had been going and now did not know where he was. He made brief eye contact with a dero, who was working a young man for the dole. "Strange," she said aloud.

When Rusty stopped turning, she quickly made her way to him, angling her approach so as to walk up behind him. At the last second, she stepped to his right, then quickly stepped in front of him.

"Can I help you," she asked.

Rusty stammered, "Um. Huh. Um."

"Sorry." She extended her hand. "Milla. Not short for Camilla."

Suddenly, Rusty stepped forward to avoid a careening rollerblader. She stepped back, prepared to strike him, but he had caught her off guard and her response was delayed enough for him take hold of her hand. She stared to jerk her hand away, but she saw in his eyes that there was no harmfulness there, and she let him steady her.

"Nice save," she said.

He touched his hat, and she worked her hand free from a longer-than-usual handshake.

He introduced himself.

She tossed out a bit that she had used many times before in Sydney, being that Rusty was such a common name. "You don't seem too Rusty to me," she said.

He took the bait, saying, "No. That's my name." She spoke her usual line, saying, "Sorry."

"You didn't name me," he said.

His response caught her off guard, and she laughed.

Rusty laughed, and Milla gazed into his eyes for a moment before he said something she only half-heard and to which she only half-responded. He knelt before her, and she removed her foot from her shoe and said something about Cinderella. *So unusual*, she thought. *This connection. Like none I have known.* He said something about Prince Charming and Cinderella. She smiled, refocused. *Back to work*, she thought.

"You seem lost," she said. "What are you looking for?" "A cheap boozer, first of all," he said.

Of course, she thought. *Just like all the rest. And now he's looking me over like they all do.*

"And to maybe sell a few diamonds to pay for some beer."

Now he's talking, she thought. *And he sure isn't asking much—just enough to pay for some beer.*

"You're in luck. I know a cheap boozer," she said. *Time to turn it on*, she thought. She leaned in close enough to brush her hair against his sun-worn cheek and whispered, half seductively, half playfully, "And I know a diamond buyer."

He cheered up at this. "Ace!" he said. "Just tell me where and who, Cinderella."

"You know The Lord Nelson?" "Never heard of him."

Milla laughed. *He really isn't from around here.* "That's the boozer," she said.

She saw his cheeks redden with embarrassment and decided to move on. "We'll meet there," she said. "And I'll introduce you to the buyer." She pulled a slip of paper from her handbag, jotted down The Lord Nelson, and hand the paper to Rusty. "In case you forget."

"How far is it?"

"Turn back the way you came—" She stopped, interrupted not only by the realization of her mistake of admitting she watched him walk this way, but also interrupted by Rusty.

"How do you know which way I came?" Rusty asked, eyeing her suspiciously.

Milla laughed nervously and longer than natural, attempting to buy time to formulate her reason for knowing which way he came from. Finally, she said, "I saw you head down here from George Street. You looked lost."

"And you stalked me." He smiled. "I've been stalked by more dangerous women than you, Cinderella, so I'll let this one slide."

"Thank you for your pardon, my lord," Milla said, mimicking a curtsy. *Oy vey, I'm such a fool for this guy.*

"So how do I get there from George Street?"

Milla gave him directions to The Lord Nelson and declined his offer to walk there with him, making an excuse to return to the office.

He touched the brim of his hat and said, "In ten or fifteen, Cinderella."

He stepped past her, and she leaned toward him slightly, almost imperceptibly, but just enough so that he had to brush against her to pass by. This was not part of her usual routine. Typically, after getting at least a little of what she wanted, she kept her distance.

She watched him walk away, and when there was enough distance between him and her, she exited the park and walked quickly back to Drago's jewelry store, all the while aware of being followed by the dero Rusty had made eye contact with and all the while wondering if they were working together.

* * *

When she turned onto Kendall, she noticed that the dero no longer followed her. She slowed down her pace and entered Drago's jewelry store. The old man sat behind the counter, studying his hands with his jeweler's eyepiece.

"So?" he asked her without looking up.

She ignored him and walked up the stairs to her office. She woke up her computer and typed Rusty's name into the search engine. Nothing. She called out to Drago, "Where did you say the Outbacker was from?"

"Lightning Ridge," Drago called back. "You get anything out of him?"

She ignored him and typed Lightning Ridge into the search engine.

She clicked on various sites, read through them quickly. Seemed to be the Opal capital of New South Wales, yet here was this guy selling diamonds in Sydney, this guy who the internet had never heard of. He didn't seem dangerous, but she was unsure of the man who had followed her, who could be working with Rusty.

She picked up her cell phone, dialed. "Alek, I need your and Mirko's services." She paused. "Yes, try to find Mirko before heading over. I could need both of you."

She hung up the phone, leaned back in her worn leather chair, and thought of Rusty, the way he smelled of old leather when she leaned in close to him. She thought of his eyes, too, so…so innocent, no harm in them. It had been a long time since she had seen innocence in the eyes of a man.

Many years ago *was the last time she had seen innocence in a man's eyes. She had been fourteen and had been caught as a stowaway on a cargo ship going to Australia. The man had found her wedged between large containers of cheese and curd, much the way the soldiers had found her wedged between the walls of her home six years earlier.*

The man said nothing, backed out of Emilija's hiding place, and returned a few minutes later with a plate of food and a bottle of water. He left without a word, and he returned the next morning with another

plate of food and a bottle of water. He watched her eat and asked her to follow him. He led her around the large containers of exports and down several flights of stairs, past the boilers, and to the lavatory.

For a moment, she did not trust him, but when he opened the door, held it for her, and pointed inside, she saw the innocence in his eyes. She entered the lavatory, closed and locked the door, did her business, and exited to find him with his back turned to the door. He turned to her, smiled, and led her back to her hiding spot several floors above where they had been.

He did this three times each day, and on several of the trips, Emilija started to tell him her story: How her family had been murdered by the Army of the Republic of Bosnia and Herzegovina during the Bosnian war, how she had been captured and sold into the worst kind of slavery, how she had escaped and had made her way by walking, hitchhiking, and stowing away to the ports of Athens, hopping a ship, any ship, to get her away from the troubles of Europe.

But he never spoke, and she never spoke. And when he led her from the ship late one night after arriving in the port of Sydney, they did not speak. Although she was young, she wanted to offer him what she had been taught to offer, but she knew he would not take it, so she did not offer it. Instead, she raised her hand in a simple wave good-bye, as he made his way back onto the ship.

* * *

Now she leaned back in her chair and thought, *That was over fifteen years ago.* She had done much since then, some of which she regretted. Most of which she didn't, because the things she had done had led her to this office where she sold the things she knew how to sell and could sell them only to those to whom she wished to sell. The buying was the other part of that, and because she was a great seller, she was a great buyer. Because she was great at both, she would not have much more use for Drago, who had been both a helpful and a cruel hand, forcing her, on occasion, to sell things she did not wish to sell. Because of this, she now saw him as only a stepping stone on the path to where she wanted to be: a woman in command of her own journey to her own destination.

Milla drifted in and out of memories and daydreams until Alek and Mirko pulled themselves up the stairs to her office almost two hours later.

She did not ask where they had been. *That is their business*, she thought. *They are here now, and these men, although not innocent men, are good men. At least to me.*

"We're going to The Lord Nelson," she said.

The men nodded.

"Stay well behind me," she said.

The men nodded.

"It's not the man I'm meeting that I'm worried about," she said. "It's the one I think is working with him. A dirty, dero-looking man. He followed me until I turned onto Kendall. I suspect he'll be waiting for me somewhere between here and The Lord Nelson."

Alek nodded.

"What do we do to him if he does something to you?"

Mirko asked.

"Whatever it takes, as usual," Milla said, as she checked her handbag for the handgun she placed in it earlier.

"Understood," Alek said.

"My favorite way of doing things," Mirko said. "The whatever-it-takes way."

"You want I should get the car?" Alek said.

"We'll walk," Milla said. "Don't want to take a chance of him seeing me step out of a car."

They walked down the stairs and were almost to the door when Drago called out, "Who are these thugs?"

"My insurance," Milla replied and pushed open the door.

"Against what?" Drago asked.

Milla turned to see Drago eyeing her suspiciously.

"Against whatever comes up," she said.

Alek and Mirko moved to each side of her and each of them clasped their hands before them, assuming the stance of bodyguards.

"You know she works for me," Drago said. "So you two work for me."

"We work for whoever the money is coming from," Alek said calmly.

"Get these thugs out of my store," Drago said. "Our store," Milla said.

"For now," Drago said. "For now," Milla said.

* * *

Before arriving at The Lord Nelson, Milla put on her best happy-go-lucky face. She expected Rusty to be upset, so to put him off guard, she sashayed into the bar. She saw him sitting in the corner, obviously drunk.

"Cinderella," Rusty slurred.

"Somebody has the wobbly boot on," she said.

"What'd you expect sending a thirsty Australian Outbacker to a bar?" He dug deep into his pants pocket, pulled out some diamonds, and dropped them on the table. "Name your price, Cinderella."

She quickly cupped the diamonds under her hand and looked around. She half-suspected that he did this to indicate to the dero he was working with that she now had the diamonds. "Rusty, you don't know the kinds of people around here." She quickly plucked the diamonds one by one from the dirty table and looked them over. "These are fine specimens."

"How would you know? You the buyer or something?" "I am." She extended her hand. "Milla the buyer. Nice to meet you."

Rusty sloppily shook her hand. "I shoulda known."

For a moment, she felt hurt, as if he thought she was the kind of woman a man like him could not trust. *I guess I am*, Milla thought. *I guess I am that type of woman.* This thought reminded her that she was not here for a good time, that she was here on business, no matter how attracted she was to the man across from her. She mentally hardened herself and began negotiations, engaging in, but quickly forgetting the chit-chat that often goes along with such a negotiation. By the end of the conversation, she had offered him two thousand dollars for the lot, turning down his low offer of nine hundred in an attempt to not only build trust in her, but to also build distrust against Drago, who she knew had offered much less for the diamonds. *Surely*, she thought, *this would keep Rusty from ever returning to Drago with business.*

After side-stepping his attempt to learn her last name and making him think that she did not know his last name, she rose from the table, put on her best pleasure-doing- business-with-you façade, and danced out of the bar, in much the same way she had danced in.

Across the street, she saw Alek and Mirko, standing with their backs against the wall of a small alley, attempting to be inconspicuous but sticking out like polished suites of armor in an abandoned castle. A moment later, her wrist was clasped, vice-like, and her mouth was quickly covered, as she was pulled into a tiny alley next to The Lord Nelson. Her abductor tossed her to the ground. She struck the ground hard, but her arms had fallen beneath her, protecting her torso from the asphalt ground. She turned over quickly, but this only seemed to expedite the speed at which her abductor was able to pin her to the ground with his foot. She immediately saw that the man above her was the dero Rusty had made eye contact with in the park.

I'm a fool, she thought. *Rusty played me, played me so well.* "What you got there in your pretty little purse?" the dero asked, pulling a large knife from his boot and slicing open the bag. "Aren't you full of supr—"

He stopped, interrupted by Alek, who seemed to Milla to be talking from a great distance. The air to her lungs and brain was slowly depleting, cut off from her by the dero's foot across her throat. The sky above her began to grow gray, and the alley began to darken prematurely.

She faintly heard a brief, tense conversation between the men, and suddenly the foot of the dero was off her neck. She lay, gasping for air, as the men scuffled around her. When she finally had enough air to move her limbs, she lunged at the dero's legs, aiding Alek and Mirko as much as she could in the struggle.

"Nice move, Milla," Mirko said.

With the little breath that was in her lungs, Milla said, "Tonight, we'll take this one down to the wharf."

Alek and Mirko lifted the dero and moved him into the deeper darkness of the alley as Milla gathered the contents of her purse. When she had finished collecting the items, she said, "Alek, stay here, since you're injured. Make sure the dero doesn't wake up. Mirko and I will be back with the car."

"Understood," Alek said, tearing a sleeve from his button down jacket. He sat beside the unconscious man and began making a tourniquet of the cloth.

* * *

When Milla and Mirko entered Drago's store, he didn't look up from the counter he seemed to polish endlessly. "You get anything?" he asked. "No," Milla said. "He wouldn't sell."

"You must be losing your charm," Drago said. "Where are the keys to the car?" Milla asked.

"In my pocket," Drago said. "For a price, you can have them."

Mirko stepped toward the counter. Milla reached out her hand. Drago dug in his pocket for the keys. "Where's your other friend?" Drago asked, eyeing Mirko.

"Prior obligations," Milla said.

"This one can't speak for himself?" Drago asked, dangling the keys from his pinky finger toward Milla.

"He speaks when he's spoken to, but all business questions go through me," Milla said, reaching to take the keys from Drago's finger.

He pulled the keys back quickly. "I'm coming with you," he said.

Milla studied him. *Why not,* she thought. *Maybe the dero will get free and kill him.*

"Let's go," Milla said. "And hurry. None of the waddling I see you do around this store all day."

* * *

When they arrived at the alley, Alek quickly rose and dragged the dero to the trunk of the car, not caring enough about being caught in this part of town to bother looking around to see if anyone was watching. Mirko assisted Alek, and they easily tossed the man into the trunk.

When they were back in the car, Drago asked, "Who was that?"

"Someone I suspect is helping Rusty," Milla said. "He attacked me after I spoke to Rusty. Must have thought I had the diamonds."

"So you pay one man for them, and another man steals them back," Drago said. "Shrewd men. I didn't expect that from Outbackers."

Me either, Milla thought, but said nothing. *Rusty certainly had me fooled.*

Alek cleared his throat loudly.

"You ok," Milla asked?

"When we were in the alley, the dero mumbled, 'Kill Rusty,'" Alek said.

Kill Rusty? Milla thought. To her, that was enough to know that the dero and Rusty were not working together and that she might be doing Rusty a favor by finishing off this dero. And even if she was not doing Rusty a favor, she was doing herself and the city of Sydney a favor by ridding the streets of one more dangerous man.

"We'll take the bum back to the store and bind him," Milla said. "When it's dark enough, we'll take him to the wharf and finish him off."

"Understood," Alek said. "A fun day," Mirko said.

"What have I gotten myself into," Drago said. "Wouldn't you like to know," Milla said.

* * *

Around midnight, Milla, Mirko, Alek, and Drago drove the dero to the wharf. When the car stopped, Alek and Mirko grabbed flashlights and walked with Milla to the back of the car.

Milla popped the trunk. Alek and Mirko shined the flashlights into the truck as much to see into the darkness as to confuse the man laying bound in the trunk.

"Make it fast," Milla said and rolled her eyes. "Drago has places to go."

Alek and Mirko lifted the limp man from the trunk. Milla leaned close over him, checking for breath. Suddenly, the dero's eyes opened, and he bucked hard, striking her mouth with his forehead.

Milla fell backward and into the water. While she fought to pull herself to the surface, she thought, *This dero got me twice in one day.* She quickly resurfaced and saw Alek reaching toward her. *Refocus before someone kills you*, she told herself.

An instant later, she was underwater again. This time with Alek on top of her. She again resurfaced quickly, just in time for Mirko to tumble on top of her. *What is going on?* she thought. *A single man, beat, bound, and stuffed in a trunk emerges to toss three people into the Sydney Harbour?*

The three Serbs pulled themselves from the water just as the dero dropped into the front seat of the car.

I never thought I would think I'm glad Drago is here, Milla thought.

The three soaked Serbs got to the car just as the dero was pulling himself out of the driver's seat. He raised his arms. "Be my guest," he said.

"We'll make sure we finish him off this time, Drago," Milla said, half smiling at the frightened man sitting in the back of the car, a loaded gun he could not control held unsteadily in his hands.

Alek and Mirko lifted the man and turned him toward the water. The man turned to Milla and mumbled something to her in such a strong Australian accent that she could not understand the words. The men quickly tossed the dero into the water. Milla, Mirko, and Alek drew their guns and fired into the water at the man who swam down and then fought to resurface ahead of the blood that rose from his chest.

As Milla watched him fight against the water, she saw him smile, then watched him sink, still smiling into the darkness that enveloped him.

"Intense," Alek said. "Totally," Mirko said. "Unbelievable," Milla said.

When the three got into the car, Drago reached beneath the passenger seat and pulled out two envelopes stuffed with cash. He handed them to Alek and Mirko. "Tomorrow we go to Lightning Ridge," he said. "And for that part of our little adventure, you two work for me."

Milla was too worn out to argue, and, besides, she thought, *if nothing else comes of it, at least I'll get to see Rusty again.*

CHAPTER 7

RUSTY IN LIGHTNING RIDGE

The events in the first section of this chapter are happening in parallel to Bruce's attempt to abduct Milla in the previous chapter.

All events in this chapter happen after Milla leaves The Lord Nelson at the end of chapter 4.

* * *

Shortly after Milla exited the bar, Rusty, forgetting in his drunkenness that he had already reserved a room at the Ritz, staggered from the table to the lobby in the hotel portion of The Lord Nelson.

"What you got?" Rusty inquired of the clerk standing stiffly behind the counter.

"Pardon?"

Rusty leaned against the counter. "What you got to sleep in?"

The clerk looked Rusty over. "Sir, we got rooms that cost two hundred per night."

"That'll do." Rusty emptied his pocket of the wad of bills Milla had given him.

"Take two for the room. One for yourself." "Sir?"

"You heard me, boy. Better snatch it before I change my mind."

The clerk timidly plucked three bills from the ball of bills Rusty had tossed on the counter. Stuffing one of the bills into his pants pocket, he said, "If you need anything, sir. Let me know."

"I need some sleep." Rusty squinted his eyes, thinking. "And a new ute. You know where I could get a ute?"

"Pardon?"

"A ute." Noticing the confusion on the clerk's face, Rusty elaborated, "It's an SUV of sorts. Not like the SUVs city folks drive. One for the Outback. Rough, tough, meant to be beat up, meant to wander. Like an old dingo…like a... like a bumbling drunk." Rusty stopped talking and looked around as if trying to figure out where he was. "You got my room key?"

The clerk handed Rusty a card.

"What do I do with this? I need a key to my room." "That is the key to your room, sir."

"I'll be a kangaroo's uncle." He looked at the front and the back of the card. "I got to get out more."

"Yes sir," the clerk replied.

Rusty looked him over. "My room?"

"That way, sir." The clerk pointed to a staircase that was once grand, but was now just a staircase.

Rusty touched the brim of his Akubra hat, nearly knocking it from his head, and headed to his room.

* * *

When he awoke the next morning to the sound of housekeeping pounding on the door, Rusty felt sorry for having ever touched his lips to a drop of the wily amber liquid. He had not taken off his clothes, had slept on top of the sheets, and had not showered since leaving Lightning Ridge, but he was ready to get back to home. He opened the door to the tiny woman who had begun to curse him through the door and handed her a hundred dollar bill before walking down the hallway to The Lord Nelson's restaurant, steering clear of the barroom. *This place has it all,* he thought. *You got the money, you'd never have to leave.*

Rusty found a seat in the corner where he could watch the television mounted in the opposite corner. Someone had turned it to 9News, Sydney's up-to-date news and weather station.

"Holy dooley!" Rusty exclaimed. He rose quickly and walked to the television. The screen showed a group of rescue personnel pulling a body from the waters of Sydney Cove.

"They'll show anything these days," a woman rasped to Rusty from the booth beneath the television screen.

"I know that guy," Rusty said without turning from the television. "At least, I used to know him."

"We all know somebody," the woman said and turned her attention to the plate of ham and eggs before her.

Rusty turned to the woman. "Stole from me years ago," he said. "Looks like he got his."

The woman looked at him suspiciously. "Where'd you say you're from?"

"Not from here, and that's where I'm headed back to," Rusty said. "I've seen too much of this town."

Without ordering the breakfast that was to cure him from his hangover, Rusty walked back to his ute, cranked its worn engine, and left Sydney behind.

* * *

Soon after leaving the city, Rusty dismissed seeing Bruce being pulled from the water as a trick his aching head and bloodshot eyes had played on him. *No way that was Bruce,* he thought. *Just memories coming back. Diamonds and opals and mining and money just weighing heavy on me. Sue was right; this stuff does take its toll.*

I'll be glad when the diamonds are gone and my pockets are fat with cash. And happy as that'll make me, I'll be happier still to dump this ute for a new one, or at least one newer than this one.

Through the Blue Mountains National Park, past the towns of Lithgow, Gilgandra, Coonamble, and Walgett, Rusty kept his eyes peeled for that perfect ute, all the while knowing that the little cash he received for the three diamonds he sold to Milla was not enough to purchase one outright. The more he looked for a ute for sale, the angrier he grew that he had not gotten the money he knew those diamonds were worth. In his mind, he would go from being proud he had shown Drago he was not a pushover to being angry that Milla took advantage of him, proving him to be a pushover. Part of him wanted to turn back to Sydney, but the image of Bruce, or who he imagined to be Bruce, and the knowledge that he would never be able to hunt down Milla, who was probably a con-artist, and the dream of selling the diamonds he had stashed in Lightning Ridge, and the excitement, yes, the excitement, of seeing Sue again kept him traveling northward toward home.

* * *

At home the next morning, Rusty rose early, put on his second best suit of clothes (his first best he had worn in Sydney), and drove down to the Blue Light Café to catch Sue before she went on shift.

When he arrived, the parking lot was empty. He backed his ute—*rusty ol' thing,* he thought—into a spot, checked his hair in the mirror, and stepped out of the vehicle. He paced the parking lot for a few minutes, checking his watch. When he saw a vehicle heading his way, he moved to the front of his ute, leaned back against it, and crossed his legs, posing obtusely for the purpose of making Sue laugh at him.

I'll pretend I stood here all night for her, Rusty thought and closed his eyes well before the vehicle backed into the spot beside him.

"Well, ain't you purdy," the man who had just stepped out of the ute beside Rusty said.

Rusty opened his eyes and laughed, slightly embarrassed. Max, the owner, the manager, and the cook at the Blue Light Café, stood in front of him, wearing a hairnet, smoking a cigarette.

"I thought you were Sue," Rusty said.

"I been called worse things." Max laughed. "She'll be in soon. Called me and said she was running behind. You coming in?"

"I'll wait here." "Alrighty, Madonna."

Rusty looked at him, questioning. "Strike a pose. There's nothing to it." Rusty shrugged.

"All you Outbackers the same. No culture." Max laughed and went inside.

Rusty shook his head. *Madonna, culture? And Max's been an Outbacker longer than I have.* He laughed to himself. *Won't find people in all the world better than the ones in Lightning Ridge,* he thought. *I must be getting old—up before dawn, waiting on a woman, getting sentimental about the people in my hometown.* Up the road, a vehicle appeared. Because the sun now sent its first rays of light across the plains, he could make out that it was Sue's ute. He closed his eyes and waited for her to pull in beside him.

When he heard her step out of the truck and close the door, he pretended to fall forward, as if he had finally fallen completely asleep. He heard her laugh, and he opened his eyes to see her smiling.

"Sue." Rusty smiled at her. "I missed you."

Sue continued smiling and huffed. "You mean you missed the coffee. I'm surprised you don't have your sidekick with you."

For an instant, Rusty thought Sue meant Milla, which caused him to break into a sweat. He opened his mouth to explain, but Sue continued without noticing.

"But that old mug is probably already out herding cattle or sheep or kangaroos or wild boars or whatever she does out thataway." Sue flipped her hand in the general direction of Kate's ranch.

Rusty laughed both at his relief that Sue didn't mean Milla and at Sue's only slightly exaggerated comment about Kate. *But how could she know about Milla?* he thought. *Stay cool*, he thought. *She'll never know about Milla.* Besides, what was there to know? That he could still almost feel the soft touch of her hand against his arm? That he could still almost smell the floral scent of her hair? That he could almost hear the light tap and shuffle of her feet as she drifted in and out of The Lord Nelson?

He snapped out of his daydream to realize that Sue had asked him a question, and that she was standing, with hands on hips, waiting for an answer. She raised one eyebrow. "Well?" she asked.

Rusty took a stab in the dark, thinking there was a good chance that she had just asked him if his trip to Sydney had gone well. Finally, he said, "Um. Yep."

"I'll take that as a committed 'yep' and not the hesitant 'yep' that it actually was." Sue turned to go inside the Blue Light Café. "Meet me here at 8. We'll take your ute to the Bath."

Stunned that Sue had asked him out instead of him asking her out as he had planned, Rusty watched her walk into the café, got into his ute, and drove away, forgetting entirely that he had gone to the Blue Light Café looking for a date *and* a cup of coffee.

* * *

Later that evening, after a day of doing little more than lazing around his pad in his boxers and socks, Rusty showered, put on his best suit of clothes, which he had made time to wash, and made himself presentable.

Showering and dressing up twice in one day, he thought. *Sue must really be under my skin*. And although he had never been much into music, especially American music, he thought of the Sinatra song, "I've Got You Under My Skin," and he wondered how Sinatra would have treated a woman like Sue…or like Milla. Would he have danced with her across the dirty floor of The Lord Nelson? Would he have taken her hand and kissed it? Touched her chin and caressed it? Or would he have stood, staring into his dunny's mirror two days later, thinking about what he should have done?

"Well, that's all over now," Rusty said to himself. "I'll never see that one again. But, Sue, she's a good one. A good Lightning Ridge girl if there ever was one."

By the time he arrived at the Blue Light Café, he had convinced himself that Sue was the one girl he couldn't live without and that the hustle and bustle of Sydney had just gotten into his head, made him think things he wouldn't otherwise think. *And made me think I saw things I didn't really see*, he thought, remembering the body he saw being pulled from the bay.

Rusty checked his watch. 7:30. Enough time to grab a cup of coffee, but not enough time to truly savor it the way he liked to do in the evenings. "I'll just wait out here," he said to himself. He closed his eyes, relaxed, and dozed off.

Fifteen minutes later, a tap on the glass woke him.

"Huh? Sue?" he said, squinting through the haze of waking.

Outside his window, a familiar face stood smiling back at him, a stray lock of blond cascaded perfectly from beneath a perfectly angled black beret. He sat up straight. "Milla?"

He opened the door quickly, too quickly, striking her with it. She staggered back and was stopped by a late model, freshly polished red-with-black-pinstriped ute that was parked behind her. Rusty jumped out to steady her, but she had already righted herself.

"We have got to quit meeting this way," she said, smiling.

"How did you find me?"

"Your beat up old ute isn't hard to find."

He laughed, nervously. "I mean here. In Lightning Ridge."

"You told me, silly," she said. "When we met. You were drunk. You told me lots of things."

He scratched his head, wished he had his Akubra hat to pull or push or somehow adjust while he thought back to that evening. He knew he "had his wobbly boot on," as Milla had put it, but he didn't remember being that wobbly. And he didn't remember telling her where he was from. Heck, he remembered he didn't even tell her his last name. "So?" she asked, pulling him from his reflections. "What are we going to do? You're dressed up for something, unless you just always sleep in your ute dressed up like that."

He laughed. *She's probably right*, he thought. *I probably had two wobbly boots on that night. Hard to tell what I told her.*

"I'm meeting a…a friend here," he said. "We're going to the Artesian Baths. Or just the Baths, as we call them." He smiled.

She smiled. "Sounds fun," she said.

"You're welcome to join us," he said. Immediately he thought, *What have I done?*

As if on cue, Sue's ute pulled into the parking lot. She parked one car down from them.

"Maybe you should, you know, come back tomorrow," he said, trying to sound smooth, but hearing the nervousness in his voice.

"But the Baths sound fun, Rusty," Milla said and playfully swatted at him.

"Yes, Rusty, they do," Sue said, as she turned the corner of what Rusty assumed to be Milla's shiny new ute. She extended her hand to Milla. "I don't believe we've met."

Milla took her hand. Milla's manicured hand against Sue's hand caused Rusty to realize how cosmopolitan Milla really was.

Rusty introduced them.

"Met in Sydney, did you?" Sue asked, looking at Milla. She turned to Rusty. "Rusty, you didn't say you met anyone in Sydney."

"Well, no, I, um, well, we haven't really talked, Sue." "We can talk on our way to the Baths," Sue said.

"That would be wonderful," Milla said. "Shall we take my ute?"

Sue turned to Milla, looked her over carefully. Her angled beret. Her crisp black business suit. Her bright red pumps. "You probably wouldn't like them," Sue said.

Milla smiled. "Quite the opposite. Rusty explained them to me, and they sound fabulous."

"Oh, he did?" Sue asked.

I did? Rusty thought. *Maybe I did. It would make sense that I did. But did I?*

"Yes," Milla said cheerfully. "And he invited me along." "Oh, he did?" Sue asked.

"I did," Rusty said. "I just thought she's in town. She's never been there. They're fun. You and me, we see each other all the time—"

Sue cut off Rusty. "We do see each other all the time. Almost too much," she said. She looked around, crossed her arms. To no one in particular she said, "I'm not going to let this ruin my evening." She turned to Rusty. "We'll go in your ute. Your friend can go in hers."

"It will be a party!" Milla exclaimed and jumped into her ute. She rolled down the windows. The radio blared techno music. "I'll follow you," she called out over the music.

Rusty made as if to touch the brim of his Akubra hat, but since he was not wearing the hat, he touched his head instead, as if making the first point of the Sign of the Cross across his body. He was too shaken to be embarrassed by this, and, without further hesitation, he climbed into his ute, closed the door, and started the engine.

"A friend," Sue said, as they were pulling out of the parking lot. "She's too hot to be a friend."

"She is," Rusty said. "I mean that she's a friend, not that she's hot."

Rusty hoped the lights from the dashboard did not illuminate his face enough for Sue to see that he was lying and that he knew that he was lying about Milla's hotness.

"Why didn't you say anything to me about her?" "We didn't talk."

"We talked this morning."

"But for just a few minutes. And I wasn't thinking about her," he lied. "I was so surprised that you asked me out that I didn't know what to say. Heck, I even left without my morning coffee."

Sue laughed. "You did forget your coffee," she said. "I even poured you some, thinking you would be in behind me."

Rusty laughed. "I hope you didn't charge me for it."

"I didn't, but I'm going to now," she said. She turned to him and said, "Why did you invite her on our date? This was supposed to give us some alone time."

"It was a mistake," he said. "I was trying to be friendly and thinking if I'm friendly she'll buy more diamonds."

"Diamonds?" Sue sat up straight. She turned to Rusty. "What do you mean by diamonds?"

"I can't say much, Sue. Just that I have some diamonds I can sell, and Milla has bought a few of them, and that I have a few more I would like for her to buy."

Sue sat for a moment, studying Rusty. Then she turned and faced forward. Finally, she said, "But this ruined our date, Rusty."

"Sue, I'm just trying to make some money. Not just for me, but maybe for us." Rusty reached out his hand to take hers.

"But I don't care about money!" she exclaimed, pounding the dashboard with the hand Rusty attempted to hold. "Why can you not see that?"

"But I do, Sue," Rusty said calmly. "I don't want to be a miner my whole life. I want to strike it rich, and I might have a chance at that if I sell all of my diamonds to the right person."

Rusty pulled his ute into the parking lot of The Artesian Baths. He turned off the ute and and turned to Sue. "Sue, don't say anything about this to anyone, not even Milla. Let's just forget about this for a while and try to enjoy the evening."

Sue thought for a moment. "Ok, fine," she said. "'Enjoy the evening.' Easy for you to say. You've got two girls fighting over you."

"When you put it like that…" Rusty smiled widely.

Sue slapped his arm. "Pig," she said, smiling. "Try not to make a fool out of yourself."

"I think it's too late for that."

* * *

The evening was much more enjoyable than even Rusty could have imagined. The girls talked about makeup and men and the recent trends in everything from shoes to physics. Rusty tried to keep up by speculating on the benefits of boots verses sneakers and by attempting to vocalize his views on the physics of the afterlife. But after failing miserably in his attempt to show how boots are superior to sneakers and in his attempt to clearly summarize his belief in the interconnectedness of everything, he simply shut up, lay back, and watched the sky become ever brighter with the light of pulsating stars.

Sometime after midnight, during one of the few silences of the evening, Sue said that it was well past her bedtime.

"Milla," Sue said, "do you have somewhere to stay?" "Yes. Thank you. Staying down on Morilla Street." "At the Chasin' Opal?" Sue asked.

Milla nodded.

"If you see a kind of heavyset girl with black hair cleaning rooms, that's my cousin," Sue said.

"I'll say hello."

"That's what I was about to warn you against. Better off saying nothing. She never shuts up."

Milla laughed. "Thank you."

"Just a local's way of looking out for you," Sue said. "Have a good night."

Rusty rose from the water. "Milla, you ok here alone?" "Fine. I'll be heading to the cabins soon."

Rusty and Sue went to their separate bathhouses and changed back into dry clothes before getting into his ute. "You want me to take you home or to your ute?" Rusty asked.

"Home. Maybe you can pick me up tomorrow to get my ute." She turned to him and smiled. "Thank you, Rusty. And I'm sorry."

"Huh?"

"Thank you for a great evening, and I'm sorry I was so harsh to you earlier."

"Um, well, ok. You're welcome and no problem."

Sue faced forward. "Turns out I needed a night out with a girl more than I needed a night out with you."

They laughed together for a moment and drove in silence until they reached Sue's home. Sue got out and walked to Rusty's side of the ute. He rolled down the window.

"Good night, Rusty," Sue said.

She leaned in, her lips slightly puckered.

Rusty leaned to her and touched her lips lightly with his.

They held the kiss for a beat, two beats, three.

Rusty was the first to pull away. "Good night, Sue," he said.

"Good night, Rusty."

He waited until she got inside before driving home.

* * *

At home, Rusty lay down without even removing his clothes. Just as he drifted off to sleep there was knocking on the door. Lightly at first. Then harder.

Rusty leapt from his bed, picked up an old cricket bat he kept between his bed and nightstand, and tiptoed to a window beside his front door. He pulled the curtain to one side and peered through the sliver of exposed glass to see who stood outside.

"What the…?"

He quickly unlocked the door and opened it. "Milla?

What are you doing here?"

"Couldn't sleep. Figured I would track you down." She smiled and answered his question before he could ask, "Again, your beat up old ute is not hard to find, especially in such a small town as this."

* * *

He laughed. "True." He looked out past her, to make sure no one was watching. *It takes only two eyes and one mouth for all of Lightning Ridge to know your business,* he thought. When he saw no one, he invited her inside and quickly closed the door.

"Coffee?" he offered, turning on lights and making a path through the clutter of clothes and newspapers strewn across the floor.

"Nothing for me," she said, looking around at his tiny home, clothes piled on furniture, stacks of dirty dishes in the sink, an assortment of mining tools and equipment stacked neatly in one corner. "Must mean a lot to you."

"Huh? Oh, yeah. Those tools are my life," he said. "My only hope at making it big." He rummaged in the sink for a coffee cup and rinsed it out.

"Those and the diamonds," she said.

"And the diamonds," he said, keeping his back turned to her. "But you've got all those now, and all I got is a couple thousand dollars."

"Listen, Rusty, about that," she said, stepping toward him. "That's why I'm here."

He turned to see her standing only feet from him. The ends of her hair hung damp around her face, and her makeup, seemingly infallible before this, had run slightly at the edges. Despite this, or perhaps because of this, she was even more beautiful. Rusty opened his mouth to speak, but he did not know what to say.

"You don't need to say anything," she said. "I just want to say I'm sorry for making a fool of you with such a poor deal."

"Well, now, Milla," he said, turning back to the sink and filling his coffee pot with water. "I did feel like a fool, but I feel like even more of one now, knowing that you knew you made a fool of me."

"If you'll trust me, Rusty, I want to make another deal with you. Right here on the spot," she said.

"Fool me once, shame on you," he said. "Fool me twice—"

"I want to trade my ute for yours," she said, tossing her keys on the counter.

He looked at the keys lying there, inviting him to touch them, to take them. He thought of the red ute, glistening under the parking lot lights earlier this evening. "It's not the color I would choose," he said.

"I thought it could remind you of the color shoes I wore when we first met," she said. She touched his arm and gently turned him toward her. Her eyes were moist, almost teary. "I'm sorry," he said. "I just didn't think much about your shoes."

"But you thought about me?"

"A little," he lied. "Just a little." He smiled.

She punched him playfully on the arm. "A little," she said. She glanced around the kitchen. "So? Where are the keys to your ute?"

"In the ute," he said. "I was hoping someone would steal it."

"No one would steal that thing," she said, smiling. "But a fool would trade for it," he said and laughed.

She punched him on the arm, harder this time. "You better watch it, Rusty. I'm not as nice as I look."

"Even Mother Theresa isn't as nice as you look," he said, gazing into her eyes.

She held his gaze and then stepped closer to him.

"Should we seal this deal?"

"We should," he said and pulled her close, feeling the heat of her body, the rhythm of her heart against him. "But I can't."

She nodded and stepped back.

"If you want the ute back," he said, picking up the keys and offering them to her.

"No. That's what I came for. Really. I just thought…" She took a deep breath. "But I understand. Sue is a good girl."

"She is good," he said. "Good night," she said.

He walked her to the door. "Good night," he said. "I hope to see you again."

"I'm sure you will," she said.

He watched her walk to his old ute, listened to the engine crank, and waved goodbye as she drove away.

* * *

The next morning, Rusty drove his new ute down to the Blue Light Café. Sue's ute was already there. He parked away from the other cars to avoid a car door inadvertently striking his ute, and he went inside.

The place was mostly empty, and Rusty sat down at his usual table. Sue immediately saw him and went over.

"I didn't see you pull in," she said.

He smiled broadly. "Let me show you why you didn't see me," he said and rose from the table.

Outside, he said, "You see that?" He pointed to the red ute parked away from the other autos.

Sue's face immediately fell, then reddened. "Milla brought you?" she asked.

"Of course not," Rusty said. "That's mine."

Sue's expression lightened. "Really? It looks just like hers. Who's open where you could get it this early?"

"No one is," Rusty said. "And it is hers. Was hers." "What? How?"

"Traded her for it. She took mine. I took hers."

Sue's face darkened. "What else did you two trade, Rusty?"

"Nothing, Sue," Rusty said. "She felt bad about the diamonds and wanted to give me something else to make it fair."

"And she gave you her ute?" Sue looked around, thinking. "That seems so strange."

"Why's that?"

"It just doesn't add up. She drives all this way to trade utes, because she felt bad about ripping you off?"

"Well, now, Sue," Rusty stammered, "she didn't rip me off. I held my own with her." He felt his face redden at the lie. Sue squinted, studying him. "I've known you for a long time, Rusty, and I know two things about you. One is that you're no good at bargaining, and the other is that you're no good at lying."

Rusty thought for a moment. "Well, Sue, if you want to know the truth, she did want me as part of the bargain."

"I knew it," Sue said under her breath. "And I told her we should—"

"What? You what?" Sue shoved Rusty away from her. "I'm done with you, Rusty. I'm done."

She turned and stormed back into the Blue Light Café.

"But I didn't," Rusty said to the empty parking lot. "I could have, but I didn't." He contemplated following Sue into the café, but he had known Sue for a long time, and there was one thing he knew about her. He knew she was like an old ute: Once she gets heated up, she takes a while to cool down.

Deciding to try to talk to her tomorrow, Rusty walked back to his ute, now covered lightly with the dust that always blanketed the town of Lightning Ridge. *You don't look so good in the daylight, he thought. But at least I can call you my own, and at least I can feel good that I showed Drago, though he'll never know it.*

As he was getting into his ute, an amazingly dust-free black car pulled up beside him. The driver's window rolled down, and a very large man leaned out.

"You live here?" the man asked in a strong Serbian accent. "I do," Rusty said, getting out of his ute. "Can I help you?"

"We are not from here, and we need good coffee," he said. "This place has some good coffee," Rusty said, leaning toward the open window. "Where you guys from?" "Melbourne," the driver said quickly.

"Alek," the passenger said, "we're not from Melb—"

The driver cut a glance at the passenger, then turned to Rusty and laughed nervously. "We travel so much," he said. "Melbourne. Not Melbourne. It's all the same, right?"

Rusty nodded. "We're all from somewhere," he said. "True. True," the man said. "We will get coffee here." "Watch out for the waitress," Rusty said. "She might be throwing things."

"We are not afraid," the driver said. "We can throw things, too."

Rusty and the two men laughed.

"G'day," Rusty said as he got into his ute.

He watched the car in his rearview mirror as he drove away. The men had not exited the car. *Strange ones*, he thought. *If they don't like being from Melbourne, they would fit in pretty good in Sydney.*

* * *

The next day, Rusty figured Sue had had enough time to cool off, or at least he had had enough time to set his mind to accept more heat from an overheated engine. He put on his clothes, not his first best or his second best, but just some clothes, and went down to the Blue Light Café to try to win Sue back over.

All this relationship work is tougher than mining, he thought. *I'm not the best at mining, but I'm a lot worse at keeping women for more than a day.*

When he pulled into the parking lot at the Blue Light Café, Sue's ute wasn't there. He went on inside. Olivia was waiting tables.

"Coffee, Olivia," Rusty said. "Couple of runny eggs, too."

Olivia brought him a cup and left the pot on the table without saying a word. A few minutes later, she dropped the plate of eggs on his table and walked away. Rusty spotted Max inside the kitchen and waved. Max pointed quickly at Olivia while she was not looking and shrugged to Rusty. Rusty nodded.

I know why she's angry, he thought. *I figured by now Max would know, too. But maybe Sue hadn't said anything to anyone other than her niece. Or maybe Olivia was just in a bad mood in general.*

He finished his coffee, poured another cup, and then finished his eggs. He took the dirty plate and cup and half- full coffee pot to the counter. He waved Max over.

"You know when Sue's coming in?" Rusty asked.

Max shrugged. "I expected her this morning, but Olivia showed up instead. I know I'm the owner, the manager, the accountant, human resources, the cook, and sometimes the waiter and busboy, but there's some things I just don't want to know about this place." He watched

Olivia wait a few tables. "Besides, Olivia is at least as good as Sue and younger and cuter, too."

A few years ago, Rusty would have agreed about Olivia being cuter than Sue, but her wishy-washy attitude had soured Rusty to everything about her except the coffee she served, and most of the time, she hadn't made the pot he was drinking. "Sue's more my type," Rusty said.

"You got it bad," Max said. "But maybe this will take your mind off it." Though Rusty showed no interest, Max continued, "Pete came in here this morning. Said he had been out to Allah's Rush."

Rusty perked up.

"I thought that would get you," Max said. "Pete said he was out stargazing or watching a meteor shower or something like that. You know how Pete is. And he saw some lights at the edge of the property, like someone wandering around, like they weren't sure where they were going."

"In a vehicle?" Rusty asked.

"I'm getting there," Max said. "Anyway, Pete turns the binoculars he uses for looking at the moon and stars and stuff toward the lights, and it looks like a few men with miner's lights on their heads just wandering around."

"Some big guys happen to come in here yesterday for some coffee?" Rusty asked.

"Why you changing the subject?" Max asked.

"Who says I am," Rusty said. He told Max what had happened yesterday, how he had made Sue mad and how the Serbs had stopped him to ask about coffee, but still hadn't left their car when he was well down the road.

"So that's why Sue's not here," Max said at the end of Rusty's story.

"That's not the point," Rusty said. "Those men—" "Seemed strange," Max said. "Yeah, they were in here.

I thought that was why Sue didn't show up today. They spooked her pretty bad. Kept asking her questions about mining and opals and diamonds and kept bringing up mines like Allah's Rush and Mulga's

Rush. Turns out it must have been you that spooked her worse than three Serbs."

"Three?"

"Two big guys and a smaller guy who looked like he didn't get out of the office much."

Rusty tapped the counter nervously. "Anybody talk to Sue today?"

"Olivia, maybe," Max said.

"Olivia," Rusty called. "You talk to Sue today?"

Olivia scowled at Rusty. "None of your business," she said.

"Olivia, this is important," Rusty said.

Olivia walked to the counter. "So was your date," she said. "You hurt Sue pretty bad showing up in that woman's new ute."

Max whistled. "You left that part out, you ol' scoundrel."

Rusty paid no attention to Max and instead held Olivia's gaze sternly. "So you've talked to her today?"

"This morning when she asked me to cover for her,"

Olivia said.

"She home?"

"Probably, Rusty. She doesn't want to take a chance running into you or that woman."

"Good," Rusty said. "Call her and tell her to stay there." "Are you going to check on her?" Olivia asked, sensing from Rusty that Sue could be in danger. "Will you check on her?"

"Call her," Rusty said. "Don't tell her I'm coming. I don't want her to leave."

Rusty tossed a ten dollar bill on the counter. "Keep the change, Olivia."

Olivia nodded and picked up the phone. "Thank you," she said.

* * *

In less than five minutes, he was knocking on Sue's door. "Sue, you in there? If so, open up, or at least say something."

"Go away!" she called out.

"I'm not going anywhere, Sue," he called through the door, "until I talk to you." He looked around to ensure no one was listening. "You could be in danger." When she didn't open the door, he took a chance: "And Milla could be in danger, too."

A few seconds later, the deadbolt unlocked, and Sue opened the door. Rusty smiled. "I knew you liked her better than me," he said. "Can I come in?"

Sue opened the door wider, allowing Rusty to step through. Her house, as usual, was spotless and tidy. She closed the door behind him and locked the deadbolt. She hugged him. "How did you know?"

"I went to see you at the café, and when you weren't there, I asked Max if he had heard from you," Rusty said. "He told me what happened yesterday, and I knew, I hoped, you would be here."

"I just didn't know what to do," she said. "Those men frightened me. Said they would be back today to talk to me at the café. If something like this happened any other time, I would tell you or Tom."

He winced noticeably at this.

"I'm sorry," she said. "I know you don't like him." "No, Sue, that's my problem," he said. "I'm just glad you have someone else to call when I'm not…haven't been…at my best."

"He's hooked on mining again," she said. "You know how you men are."

Rusty nodded.

"I didn't have anyone else to call, so I called Olivia to cover me and blamed my staying home on you," she said.

"A believable story," he said, and smiled awkwardly.

She smiled. "We have a history that made my story easy to believe." She walked to the kitchen. "And about Milla—"

"I'm sorry, Sue," Rusty said.

"No, I'm sorry," Sue said. "She stopped by here yesterday in your old ute. For a moment, I thought it was you coming to apologize, but then I know how you know me and that you would know it would take me a day or more to cool off."

Rusty laughed.

"She came to apologize for messing up what we had just started or restarted or whatever," Sue said, brushing a lock of hair from her eyes. "She told me what happened. She told me about your deal in Sydney, how she had made you look like a fool—"

"Hey, now," Rusty said.

Sue smiled and continued, "She said she came here to make it up to you by doing no more than trading utes, but then she saw you with me and how we were, and then there were the Baths and the stars, and things just got out of control."

"Almost out of control," Rusty said.

"Almost," Sue said. "And she told me she was immediately heading back to Sydney or at least going as far as your old ute would take her."

Rusty thought for a moment. "So she's not in danger?" "Not that I know of," Sue said. "She's probably back in Sydney by now, unless she broke down in your ute and dingos ate her."

"Why did you let me in when I said Milla might be in danger, too?"

"Because I like her better than you," Sue said and laughed. "Now that we're through worrying that someone might be on their way to the bottom of a shallow grave, do you want some coffee?"

"I had some at the café, but I think Olivia might have spit in it," he said. "So I'll take a cup."

"It's understandable why you thought I could be in danger, but why would you think Milla would be in danger?" Sue asked.

Rusty told Sue about the men yesterday in the parking lot, and he told her about Pete seeing men at Allah's Rush.

He retold her what she already knew, what she had been a participant in with the two large men and one small man from Sydney.

"So how does that put Milla in danger?" Sue asked.

"I had first tried to sell my diamonds to a man named Drago, who matches the description of the small man who harassed you in the café yesterday," Rusty said.

"You left that part of your Sydney trip out," Sue said.

Rusty continued, "Drago expected me to come back with the diamonds, but I didn't. Somehow, he found out that Milla, an up-and-coming jewelry dealer, had purchased them from me, and he followed her here."

"Why follow someone all the way from Sydney to Lightning Ridge?" Sue asked.

"Why not?" Rusty asked. "What better place to murder someone and dump a body? And you might even find more diamonds while you're here. Especially if the person you're following is a beautiful woman who knows how to make men talk."

It was Sue's turn to wince noticeably.

"Sorry," Rusty said

Sue shook her head. "Go on," she said.

Rusty continued, "You let her run around a little, get people to talk a little, and then kidnap her and make her talk."

"Did you tell her anything?" Sue asked. "I didn't," Rusty said. "Did you?"

Sue shook her head.

"Then maybe that's why they let her go back to Sydney,"

Rusty said.

"If she made it that far," Sue said. "I haven't spoken to her since she left."

"Do you have her number?" "I don't. Do you?"

Rusty shook his head.

"You do business with someone, and you don't have their number?"

"No one was supposed to know about this," Rusty said. "So much for that," Sue said. "Half of Sydney or Melbourne or wherever those people are from are crawling around here harassing people, sneaking around in the dark, trading utes."

Sue poured Rusty a cup of coffee. Rusty sipped his coffee, as they both stood silently in the kitchen.

"Ah-ha!" Sue cried out. "The ute! It has to be registered. I'll ask Eloise down at the transportation department to run its registration."

* * *

Thirty minutes later, Eloise asked Sue and Rusty, "That your gal?" as she handed over a piece of paper with the ute's VIN listed above the registered owner's name:

Emilija Novak 59 Kendall Ln Sydney, NSW

"That address," Rusty said, "seems familiar." Suddenly, his face emptied of all color. He opened his wallet and pulled out the scrap piece of paper on which he had scribbled Drago's address:

59 Kendall Ln Sydney, NSW

"What is it?" Sue asked.

Rusty didn't answer because he couldn't hear her over the beat of his own heart or over the question now looming in his head: *How am I going to tell Kate?*

CHAPTER 8

THE GAME

While Rusty tried to figure out what to tell Kate, he drove out to Mulga's Rush to pick up some more diamonds, all the while replaying in his mind his meetings with Milla or Emilija or whoever she was. The more he thought about it, the more sense it made that she had followed him from Drago's jewelry store, had acted on Drago's behalf, had learned from Drago that Rusty lived in Lightning Ridge, had shown up in Lightning Ridge, found him out, and pointed out Rusty's whereabouts to Drago and the two thugs driving him around.

As he thought about what Milla had done to him, Rusty's emotions transitioned back and forth between an anger that pounded in his head to a sick, sad feeling deep in his stomach. He had not felt this kind of sadness since he was thirteen years old when Sally, his first girlfriend, had broken up with him, turned away from his offerings of tiny opals (the first he had ever mined) by a tall, heavyset boy named Butch, who liked to cuss, chew tobacco, and pretend to toss insects into the hair of pretty girls like Sally. *Women*, he thought, *I never could keep one.*

When he arrived at his pad at Mulga's Rush, Rusty knew something was amiss before he even stepped foot out of his ute. Approaching the door, it didn't take a detective to realize that the door had been kicked in near the doorjamb and that the deadbolt had been blown off by a high caliber gun.

Whoever tried to kick it in underestimated that reinforced doorjamb I put in not long after I moved out here, Rusty thought. He pushed open the door and walked in. *Stupid. Stupid,*

Rusty thought, standing there in the open. *I'm guessing no one's still here, or I probably wouldn't be.*

He glanced around the one room shack. Everything was as it was expected to be in a situation like this. The few pieces of ragged furniture that filled the room were turned over. A tiny lamp he had purchased years ago at a yard sale had been busted. His cot had been stripped and tossed across the tiny room.

After studying the mess for a moment, a wave of nausea rolled over him. Feeling sick, he rushed out the door to the one-holer loo behind his shack and quickly sat down. *What am I thinking?* he thought.

"Apparently very little," he said, rising, pants down, to check thoroughly for the dangerous red spiders that frequently hid beneath the toilet seat. Satisfied that his search found nothing, he sat back down on the toilet.

When his eyes adjusted to the few shadows the shrubbery threw across the area, he spotted two items that were out of place—the first was that the hand-towel he usually kept wadded on a small makeshift table next to the toilet had been neatly folded, and the second was that a business card was lying face down beneath the table.

Ha. I got you now, Rusty thought as he leaned forward off the toilet. He flipped it over:

Lightning Ridge District Bowling Club
The Home of the Black Opal
Outback Entertainment Center
Call us to book your next special event!
OR
Check out our webpage for a schedule of events!

Rusty knew the place. He had several buddies from high school who still worked the tables and ran some of the events. When he was doing particularly well, he would even visit the place himself. Great food, entertainment, and prize money. And there was that cute little waitress. What was her name?

Rusty shook his head. *Getting sidetracked,* he thought. *Seems easier and easier to do these days. No opal mining, no focus. And with these diamonds burning a hole in my pocket, I've got even less focus. And then there's Milla...or was Milla. And Sue. And what was the name of that girl at the Bowling Club?*

"Nevermind," he said to himself. "What's more important is why this card is here. Did whoever ransack the place leave it as an invitation, a clue? But why leave it on the ground?"

Doesn't matter, he thought. He checked his watch. 11:15. Nevel would be at the club by now. He would give him a call and see if he had noticed anyone suspicious hanging around the club.

After finishing his business, Rusty walked back to his shack, rummaged through the mess for the old cell phone he kept out here in case of an emergency, and when he found it, dialed the club and asked for Nevel. After the preliminaries, Rusty asked, "You notice anyone from out of town hanging around the club last night?"

"Was there anyone from in town at the club last night would be the better question," Nevel replied. "Had one of those celebrity look alike concerts. You know how that brings them in from all over. Even heard one guy say he was all the way from Come By Chance."

Rusty tried to sound interested. "That so? That's a little more than a skip away." He paused. "You hear anyone say if they were from Sydney?"

"Sydney?" Nevel laughed. "Who'd be crazy enough to drive all the way from Sydney to watch a few wannabes act like who they wanna be?"

Rusty laughed. "I just wondered if there was anyone from that far away."

"None that I know of, but maybe tonight," Nevel said. "We've got that concert going again, but you know what really brings 'em in."

In unison they said, "Kangaroo butt," and laughed together for a minute.

"Never gets old," Nevel said. "You remember when we came up with that?" He didn't wait for Rusty to answer. "Me, you, and Jimmy Rogers after graduation smoking those homemade cigarettes Jimmy had stolen from his dad and watching a few 'roos hopping around Lunatic Hill."

Rusty laughed to remain polite, but he had no time for reminiscing. "Listen, Nevel, I gotta—"

But Nevel was lost in the memory. "Looking down in that canyon, you said, 'There's nothing down there, so what keeps brining these crazy opal miners back here?' And without missing a beat, Jimmy says, 'Kangaroo butt.'" Nevel laughed loud into the phone and started to cough— too many years smoking those homemade cigarettes.

Rusty chuckled. "Those were the days," Rusty said. "There's someone at my door," Rusty lied. "I better go."

"Okie dokie. Say hi to Sue for me," Nevel said as he hung up the phone before allowing Rusty to say anything. Same thing he'd done for years to turn a sad, sorry situation into a running joke.

Years ago, Sue had nearly broken up Nevel and Rusty's friendship, and she didn't even know it. Heck, at the time, Rusty didn't even know it. He had gone on a date or two with Sue, and while talking to Nevel over the phone one day, Rusty had told Nevel about Sue. Nevel immediately fell silent, which was completely out of character. Rusty listened for a moment, listening hard to what he thought was sobbing from the other end of the line. Before he could say anything, Nevel said, "Say hi to Sue for me," and hung up the phone.

Later, Sue told Rusty that Nevel had had a huge crush on her for many years, but that she had no interest. He never told Sue about the awkward conversation with Nevel, and he never told Nevel that Sue had told him about Nevel's crush on her. Some things were just better kept to yourself, Rusty figured.

Rusty stuffed the card into his pocket, walked over to the corner where his mining tools lay in a heap, picked up a worn but well cared for shovel, and walked out the door to a thicket of shrubs growing northwest of his home. While digging just inside the edge of the thicket, he studied the Bowling Club card in his mind, flipping it over and over, as if searching for clues. But, really, he knew the answer to the question he had called to ask Nevel. He knew who from out of town had been to the Bowling Club and who had dropped this card near the table next his toilet either before, during, or after ransacking his shack. He knew the answer, but he didn't want to know the answer. It would just tell him how much trouble, no, danger, he could be in.

He finished digging and pulled a small tin can from the dirt. He dusted it off and removed the lid. From the bottom of the can, the collection of diamonds shimmered up at him as if they produced their own light. He plucked four of the beauties from the others, closed the lid, and reburied the can. He placed the diamonds in his pocket, and now that their iridescence no longer had him transfixed, he returned to contemplating how much danger he could be in.

He figured that if someone could be so hard set on getting more diamonds from him that they would not only send a pretty woman to follow him around Sydney, send her seven hundred and thirty kilometers to mine him for information, and show up on their own to have a look around, but would also take it so far as to break into his shack, then how dangerous could these men be? Heck, how dangerous could Milla be? Obviously, she was dangerous enough to do business with these men, but, again, how dangerous could these men be?

* * *

Hey, look at it, Alek," Mirko said, leaning out the window of the late model Holden Caprice. He pushed a two and a half foot long stick into the mouth of copper- colored snake that lunged at him repeatedly.

Alek didn't look. Instead, he worked on loading the cartridge of his Taurus 1911, and he worked hard, since the thickness of his fingers caused him to fumble with each bullet before sliding it into place.

"Alek, look," Mirko called out. He had the stick up to window level with the snake coiled tightly around it. "I think it's mad."

Drago leaned over to see what Mirko held. "Idiot," Drago said. Even though his vision was not what it once was and he could barely distinguish stick from snake even at this distance, Drago knew what kind of snake it was. "Drop it. That's a mulga snake."

"But I think he likes me, boss," Mirko said, slowly pulling the stick and the snake closer to the open window.

"He likes you dead," Drago said.

Suddenly, an excruciatingly loud blast rang from Alek's direction and the snake disappeared, along with most of the stick that Mirko was still holding.

"What'd you do that for?" Mirko asked.

Drago reached calmly across the back of the seat, took the loaded gun from Alek's hand, and sat back in his seat. "If either of you wake me again before Emilija gets here, I'll blow you both away like the snakes that you are." He lay the seat back, the length of the car, and the shortness of his stature allowing him to nearly stretch out fully. He lay the loaded gun on his chest and the day's newspaper over his face.

"Now look what you did," Mirko said.

Alek closed his eyes and pushed himself into the corner of the backseat.

"That her?" Mirko asked Alek a moment later.

"That's a motorcycle," Alek said. "You know she's driving that beat up old thing."

"It's called a ute," Drago said. "And I don't want to hear another word about what she's driving or what she was driving."

"You sore that she gave her ute away to that bushwhacker?" Mirko asked.

Drago didn't answer.

"Why does no one ever answer me?" Mirko asked. "Because you're stupid," Alek said. "Shut up and watch for Emilija and her rusty heap of rattling junk." Alek leaned forward so that he could see Drago grimace. Alek smiled. "I'm getting some shut eye," he said.

Fifteen minutes later, Milla pulled off the road and drove slowly into the clump of trees that Mirko had somehow maneuvered the Holden into. When she pulled up beside them, the ute backfired, coughed, and shut off. Milla rolled down her window and said, "Wonderful piece of machinery." She smiled at Drago, who was now sitting up and gazing at her angrily.

He leaned over to talk to Milla through Mirko's open window. "What have you found?"

"Nothing more than I've told you already," Milla said. "Rusty's young woman wouldn't tell me anything yesterday, although I all but made her my best friend. She's either playing dumb, or she really is dumb. Probably the latter, considering her taste in men."

Milla turned to look over her shoulder in time to see the backend of a ute drive down the highway. *Backward Outbacker has no idea a couple autos were hidden here,* she thought.

"How about the old woman?" Drago asked. "She scares me," Milla said.

Mirko laughed.

"I dare you to try her," Milla said, studying Mirko. She turned back to Drago. "I only saw her from a distance yesterday and this morning, and I don't want to see her any closer. I tramped around her place last night, looking for anything I could find, but I couldn't get close to her house because of those dogs she keeps."

Drago nodded. "I left your man an invitation at his place outside of town."

Milla studied Drago, waiting for an explanation.

"A business card for a local club," Drago said. "He'll want to know who tore up his place, and he'll come looking for whoever left that card behind."

"If you wrecked his place, how is he going to find the card?" Milla asked.

"I put it where everyone goes eventually," Drago said. "Left it on a wadded up towel where he does his business."

Alek glanced in the rearview mirror and swallowed hard. "You sure, Drago? I folded that wadded towel." "You, huh? What?" Drago asked.

"I had to go, and then I wiped my hands with the towel," Alek said. "My mama always told me to fold any towel neatly and place it where it goes. I never saw the card."

Milla laughed. "Hardened criminals you guys are. A homemaker, a jeweler, and an idiot."

"I'm not a jeweler," Mirko said, straight-faced.

The three of them looked at him, waiting for him to smile at his joke. When he didn't, Milla continued, "So now you don't know if he'll be there or where he'll be."

Drago smiled. "My love, I had an after-market tracking device added to the ute. You didn't think I would give you a brand new ute because I trusted you?"

Milla looked as if she had just been struck, but then quickly regained her composure. "Then why bother with the card if you could just track him down?"

"This way, he meets us on our terms and in a public place," Drago said. "Emilija, you are cute, and you are cunning, but you have a lot to learn about men like your Outbacker. Men like that don't want to make a ruckus in their own hometown. Especially a little place like Lightning Ridge where everybody knows everybody's business."

Milla thought for a moment. Not only was she cute and cunning, but she was smart enough to know when she had just been taught an important lesson. She nodded, then said, "This is good, but it seems like I'm done here. No matter how much of a simpleton Rusty is, I think it's best that he does not associate me with you and Tweedledee and Tweedledum."

"Why's that, 'Milla?'" Drago asked, emphasizing her Australian name. "Do you have other plans for you and your Outbacker?"

"I could," Milla said. "If we ever want to do business with him again, I can't be associated with you, because after this, you are likely to be out of the picture. But he has no idea I'm part of this, so he's likely to deal with me again. And if he doesn't, there's a good chance his young woman will if she ever gets her hands on anything worth selling."

Drago nodded. "You truly are cunning."

"And cute," Milla said, rolling up her window.

The three Serbs watched as she started Rusty's old ute, drove slowly out of the clump of trees, and turned in the direction of Sydney. When she was out of site, Mirko turned around to Alek and said, "She called you dumb."

Drago shook his head and spoke to Alek, "I'm going to sleep. I suggest you do the same, Tweedledum." He turned to Mirko. "Wake us if you see anything suspicious or if anyone seems to be slowing enough to see us back in these trees." To both of them, he said, "We'll go to the Bowling Club tonight, get there before the Outbacker does, and be waiting for him at a table when he gets there. See what kind of offer we can make him."

When Drago awoke, the interior of the car was nearly dark. He leapt from his reclined position. "Mirko," he shouted.

Mirko woke up slowly, rubbed his eyes. "We there yet?" he mumbled.

"You were supposed to wake us up," Drago said.

Mirko immediately started the car.

"Alek, you awake?" Mirko said, as he eased the car out of the stand of trees and onto the road.

Alek didn't answer. Instead, he pushed himself further back into the seat and closed his eyes.

The sun was setting, so it was not as late as Drago had thought.

Still, it was later than he had imagined in his plan to deal with the Outbacker. He hoped that the Outbacker was not there, but he was almost sure that he would be. A man like the Outbacker would be nervous and would show up early to get the confrontation over with, even if it meant pacing the floor waiting for the other party, which is what a man like this wanted, to arrive before the other party, which is why Drago wanted to be at the Bowling Club earlier than they would be now. *Such a game*, Drago thought. *I could have just been a jeweler. That's what my mom wanted and what her dad had been.*

Drago watched the tall Eucalyptus trees and the squat Golden Wattle shrubs blur past his window. *But now I'm more than a jeweler. Or am I less than a jeweler? I guess it depends on how you cut it. So much like a diamond, this life. Cut it this way, and it's a little brighter. Cut it that way, and it's a little darker. Rotate it, study it, and cut it again, and it becomes a little different.*

He thought about the men he rode with. Tweedledee and Tweedledum. He smirked. Did that make him Alice? He certainly felt like Alice at times. This was one of those times. He imagined that instead of flying horizontally across plains into the darkness he was falling into the darkness, down the rabbit hole.

He drifted between non-sensical and sensical thoughts until they pulled into the parking lot at the Bowling Club. The lot was full of cars, utes, and even an ATV or two. He scanned the parking lot for Emilija's red ute. When he saw it parked at the far end of the parking lot, his heart skipped a beat. *This never gets old,* he thought. *I never get used to it, the uncertainty, the danger.*

* * *

Rusty watched from his ute as the Holden Caprice pulled into the parking lot and the two large men and Drago walked into the club. He would let them get situated, maybe even give them time to get a drink or two, then go inside, ask them if they had lost something, then toss the card down.

They would stare at him for a moment. Drago would speak first. "I don't know what you mean," Drago would say.

Rusty would say, "I mean this." He would pick up the card and toss it in Drago's face.

The two big men would be dumbfounded that Rusty would treat their boss in this way. "Hey," they would say. "Hey this," Rusty would say and turn the large round table over into their laps. A fight would ensue, a fight more characteristic of a bar fight than a bowling club fight, but a fight all the same. Rusty would clean the floor with the men. The authorities would be called to arrest the Serbs, and Rusty would watch them being hauled away in the back of a police car. Sue would be there watching with him. Or Milla. Or maybe that cute waitress who works at the Bowling Club.

Rusty pulled himself from his daydream and checked the time. 8:30. Good enough. They had been inside for 15 minutes, and he was ready to get this over with. He exited the ute and walked inside.

Inside, he immediately saw them sitting at a long table from which two couples just got up. The three men sat eating, focused intently on their meals. *So much for turning a large round table over in their laps*, Rusty thought. As he approached the table, Rusty grew nervous and put his hand in his pocket, fingering the card.

Drago was the first to see him. He rose quickly and extended his hand. "My friend," he said, smiling.

This is not going as planned, Rusty thought. *I'll shake like a civilized man.*

Rusty pulled his hand from his pocket to shake Drago's hand. Due to the sweat on his palm, the business card stuck to his hand and then fell on the table, face down. The men shook.

"What's this?" Drago said, spotting the slightly crumpled card on the table.

"It's what I came here for," Rusty said.

"Have a seat," Drago said, extending his hand to the one across from him, the one closest to Rusty. "What is this?" he asked again.

"You know what it is," Rusty said, sitting down. He picked up the card to turn it over, revealing one of the four diamonds that he had stuffed in his pocket at Mulga's Rush. Rusty gasped and tossed the card back over the diamond. He looked at Drago, hoping he had not seen the diamond, although he knew he had. He imagined that everyone in the club had.

"I saw what you have there," Drago said. "How much?" "Just the one," Rusty said too quickly. He cleared his throat. "Just one."

"Allow me to rephrase," Drago said. "How much for everything you have in your pocket."

Rusty said nothing. He felt trapped, unsure what to say, how much to say. He felt he had said too much already.

"Thirty thousand?" Drago asked.

Rusty felt his eyebrows raise uncontrollably.

"Forty thousand?" Drago asked. He smiled.

Rusty cleared his throat. "That's a start," he heard himself say.

Without taking his eyes off Rusty, Drago said to Alek, "Go get fifty thousand out of the car. That's my final offer, Outbacker."

Rusty did not speak, only nodded. He saw himself raise his hand and shake Drago's. He felt his hand dig into his pocket for the other three diamonds. He watched as he lay them gently on the table and cover them smoothly with the crumpled business card.

"I'm taking your word, Outbacker," Drago said, "that I'm getting a fair deal. For all I know, you could have just laid buttons on the table. My eyes aren't what they once were."

Alek walked back in and passed an envelope to Rusty.

Rusty opened it slightly.

"This is a gentlemen's deal," Drago said. "No need to count it. It's all there." He smiled. "See? I trust you. You trust me."

Rusty nodded, unbuttoned a single button in the middle of his shirt, put the envelope in his shirt, and buttoned his shirt.

Drago looked around. "You go on out first, Outbacker.

I'll give you time to go your way. Then I'll go mine."

Rusty rose and walked out the door to his ute. He sat down inside the ute, closed the door, and locked it. He pulled the envelope from his shirt and opened it, flipping through the bills quickly. *If this isn't fifty thousand dollars,* he thought, *it's pretty darn close.*

He held the envelope in his hands for a moment, then set it in his lap. He stared ahead and started to smile, then to laugh. *Fifty thousand for four diamonds,* he thought.

"Fifty thousand for four diamonds," he said. "Fifty thousand for four diamonds!" he shouted. He took a deep breath. "Okay," he said. "Okay."

He bent to place the envelope under his seat. Just as he did, he heard a heavy thump on his passenger's side window. He jerked and turned in that direction, wrenching a muscle in his back.

Alek struck the window with his fist. A small spider web of cracks started to form. He struck it again. To Rusty's right, another loud thump. He turned to see Mirko striking the driver's side window. Drago was hobbling across the parking lot toward Rusty's ute. His fist was in the air, and he was shouting, although Rusty could not hear what he was saying.

Suddenly, he could hear what he was saying, because Alek had broken through the passenger window and was now straining to get his hands on Rusty.

"Four lousy diamonds," Drago shouted. "Four lousy diamonds! Where are the rest of my diamonds?"

Alek's arms flayed inside the vehicle, reaching for Rusty. Finally, Rusty thought to start the ute. He dug for his keys, shoved them into the ignition, and cranked. The engine started up smoothly just as Mirko shattered the driver's side window. He quickly reached in and grabbed Rusty by the shirt, then the arm, then the neck. Rusty pushed hard on the gas, and the ute lunged forward, but for only a moment. Mirko had a tight enough grip on Rusty that when the ute moved forward, Mirko pulled Rusty halfway through the window.

Before he knew it, Rusty was outside the ute and was on the ground with Mirko on top of him.

"I want some of that," Alek said.

"You got the bum," Mirko said. "This one is mine." He turned back to Rusty and raised his fist.

Rusty grimaced, waiting for the blow. From the direction of the Bowling Club, several men began to shout. Rusty watched as the men, with Nevel in the lead, ran across the parking lot toward him.

Mirko jumped off him. Alek picked up Drago and slung him over his shoulder, as if he were a little boy. The three men ran toward the Holden and jumped in, just in time to avoid the mob of men who were now beating and kicking the once pristine automobile.

Rusty rose and dusted himself off. He watched as the Holden sped away, and then he made his way to his still- running ute and turned it off. By the time he had done this, Nevel was standing at his side.

"You hawking bad opals again?" Nevel asked, smiling. "You know me," Rusty said, "always looking for a quick buck."

"I saw you in the club, and it looked like some trouble," Nevel said. "Been watching for you all day. Not like you to call and not want something."

"Am I really that bad?" Rusty asked, slightly hurt by the comment that he knew to be true.

Nevel shrugged.

"Thanks for saving me," Rusty finally said. "Those guys would have made me unrecognizable."

"You almost are, driving around in that new ute," Nevel said. "Well, was-new ute."

Rusty laughed. "Yeah, well, I don't like to have nice things."

"Then you shouldn't be with Sue," Nevel said. He smiled awkwardly, turned his back to Rusty, and walked back toward the club.

"I'll tell her you said hi," Rusty called after him.

Nevel raised his hand.

In the darkness, Rusty couldn't tell if Nevel was waving or if he was showing him exactly what he thought of him.

CHAPTER 9

RUNNING OFF THE SERBS

Nevel says hi," Rusty said to Sue after she opened the door to her house.

"Oh my gosh," Sue said. "Did he do this to you? Why would he have done this to you?"

"Done what?" Rusty asked, looking himself over.

Sue grabbed his arm, pulled him into her house, her bedroom, and stood him in front of the full-length mirror behind her bedroom door. "That," she said, pointing to Rusty's neck.

He lifted his chin, exposing his already bruised neck.

"Wow. I didn't know it was that bad." "Were you two fighting over me?"

"Why would we fight over you?" Rusty put too much emphasis on "you" and immediately felt bad. He glanced over his shoulder in time to see Sue wince, but he said nothing.

"Then what was it about?"

"It wasn't Nevel." He turned to look at her. "It was the Serbs."

Sue covered her mouth. Rusty noticed her hand was dry and cracked from washing dishes. He thought of Milla's hand, touching him softly on the shoulder in Sydney.

Was Milla there?" Sue asked, seemingly reading Rusty's mind.

"Why would she be?"

Sue hesitated, then stammered, "I, well, I talked to my cousin who works at the Chasin' Opal."

Rusty sighed, "Evie?" He rolled his eyes. "You want to hear this or not?"

"Half the stuff she says is lies."

"Well, Rusty, it's not about her lying or not lying this time. It's about what I saw." Sue stopped, waiting for Rusty's apology.

She waits for an apology for this but not about me asking why two men would want to fight over her? Rusty thought. When Sue continued to wait, Rusty apologized.

Sue continued, "I headed out to her place on Castlereagh Highway. Tiny place way out in the bush. But before I got there, I spotted your ute turning into some trees."

Rusty's eyes widened slightly. "Go on," he said.

"For a second, I thought it was you, you had that junker for so long. Then I remembered who it was, so I slowed down until it was in the trees. When it was pretty much concealed from the road, I picked up my speed and drove on past, but slow enough so I could see what the ute was doing." Sue took a deep breath. "It was parked there with a black Holden. I could easily see the men who kept asking me questions yesterday. When I saw that, I picked up my speed and drove on past. You know there's no good way to Lightning Ridge from Evie's, so I did end up driving to there and listening to her until it got dark enough to drive on home. Been here not more than an hour."

Rusty swallowed hard and winced at the pain that had started to creep up toward his jaw and down toward his clavicle. Strangely enough, in his chest he felt the same thing, as he realized for certain that Milla was more than she had claimed to be and that he meant less to her than she claimed him to mean. Rusty glanced around Sue's bedroom, all perfectly kept, except the bed, precisely turned down, awaiting its sleeper.

"And Evie gave me this," Sue dug in her pants pocket and handed Rusty a business card.

Emilija Novak, Jeweler, Broker

Your Personal Local and International Jewelry Broker Visit or call me for any and all of your jewelry needs! 59 Kendall Ln

Sydney, NSW Mobile: 0491 570 157

"Looks like she's legit," Rusty said.

"At least some of the time," Sue said. She crossed her arms, studied Rusty.

"Well?" Rusty asked.

"Well?" Sue responded. "You still in love with her?" "I never said I was in love with her."

"I've known you long enough to know when you're in love." Sue looked down at her feet, took a deep breath, and looked back up at Rusty. "Now what to do about that."

"Not something there to do anything about."

"I mean about that," Sue said, raising her eyebrows and nodding at Rusty's neck.

"Oh, that," Rusty turned back to the mirror. "It's nothing."

"Something's always nothing to you," Sue said. "That's how I always know what you're really saying—whatever you say is the exact opposite of what is."

Rusty smiled crookedly at Sue's reflection over his shoulder. "Then this is something, so let's forget about it." He turned to her. "Or let's remember it, make a big deal about it, celebrate it."

"I'm not laughing," Sue said, crossing her arms. "While you tell me about why those men almost pulled your head off, I'll get some ice."

In the kitchen, Sue bagged some ice, while Rusty gave an abbreviated, somewhat altered version of what happened at the Bowling Club.

When he finished, Sue tapped the table, bit her lip, looked him straight in the eyes, and said, "We need a plan."

"For what?"

"To get them out of Lightning Ridge."

"They're gone," Rusty said. He slid the bag of ice to the back of his neck, which had suddenly grown stiff and sore. *Maybe that beast did almost pull my head off,* he thought.

"Gone for now," Sue said, standing. "But if I learned anything about those men from talking to them, it's that they are determined. Unless they're beat hard and beat bad, they'll be back."

"What do you suppose we do?"

"I got an idea," she said. She grabbed her dining table chair, turned it around, and sat down, straddling it like Arthur Fonzarelli.

"Ayy," Rusty said, smiling and flipping up his collar.

Sue stared at him.

"Sorry," Rusty said. "Go ahead, 'Fonz."

"Ugh," Sue said, rising. She turned her chair back to the table. "I'll sit prim and proper like your Sydney girl."

Rusty rolled his eyes. "Whatever. What's your plan?"

She leaned in, as if there were a room full of people who could be listening and presented her plan to Rusty, who simply listened, nodded, smiled, and nodded some more.

"Fair dinkum," Rusty said when she finished. "I think it'll work."

* * *

The next morning, Rusty dialed the number on Milla's business card.

"Milla?" Rusty asked when the phone on the other end of the line was answered, but no one responded.

"Rusty?" Milla asked.

"The one and only," Rusty said, smiling into the phone. "How did you get my number?"

"You gave it to me," he lied. "Must have been when you had the wobbly boot on."

"I don't drink, but I'll go along," Milla said.

Rusty could hear in her voice that she wasn't smiling. "Um, well, you did," he said. He grimaced. *Drop it, you dope,* he thought. "Um, anyway, I got to thinking, maybe our ute trade wasn't a fair deal, and I felt bad, so—"

"I already used that one, Rusty," Milla said. "What do you really need?"

His mind jumped from possible response to possible response. He was not good in these kinds of situations. *Why did I let Sue talk me into this? What was I thinking?*

"I don't know," Milla said. "What were you thinking?" "Huh?"

"You said, 'What was I thinking?'" "I did?"

"You did," Milla said. "What were you thinking?"

Rusty swallowed hard, wincing at the pain, much worse this morning. "I got me some diamonds that are causing me more trouble then they're worth. I got to get rid of them."

"Why would you call me?" Milla asked. "You know I'm just a one woman show. I told you that when we met."

"I'll make you an offer you can't refuse," Rusty smiled awkwardly into the phone.

"You're too desperate, Rusty," Milla said. "I have to go." "I'll go to Drago," Rusty blurted into the phone. *Oh, no,* he thought. *This was not part of the plan.*

"Then go," Milla said. "He was going to give you less that I did."

"How would you know that?"

"Huh, what?" Milla cleared her throat.

Rusty smiled to himself. For once, he had someone reeling in a verbal sparring match. "How do you know he was going to give me less than you did?"

"Everybody in Sydney knows he buys low and sells high," Milla said. "I'm just trying to break even."

Feeling confident, Rusty decided to go along with her. "But someday you want to do more than break even, right? Maybe Drago's share of the Sydney market and the surrounding market is the way to go."

Milla said nothing.

"How about it, Cinderella? Meet me at my place at Mulga's Rush tonight. Alone," he said.

"Where's that?" Milla asked.

Rusty knew she knew where his shack was. "I can't tell you, but I know you'll find it." He hung up the phone.

"Yes," he said to himself, then swung at the air like an out of practice prize fighter. "Yes," he said again, keeping his voice low to be sure not to wake Sue, who was still asleep in the other room.

* * *

When Sue awoke, they drove to the Blue Light Café for coffee. Sue poured a cup for her and a cup for Rusty. "You think your friend needs a refill?" Sue asked, nodding in the direction of Kate, sitting alone at the other side of the room.

Rusty took a deep breath. "Yeah. I'll take it to her."

By the time Rusty reached Kate's table, he was shaking so bad the coffee was nearly splashing from the pot. Kate didn't look up from her eggs. Rusty refilled Kate's mug without asking if she needed more.

"Heard you got into some trouble," Kate said without looking at him.

"A little, you know. You know how it is," Rusty said. He cleared his throat and looked around.

"I'm going to assume it was for opals and that you'll take care of it," Kate said, chewing her eggs.

Rusty turned to go.

"Rusty," Kate said.

"Yeah, Kate," Rusty said, hoping she was going to offer her help to get him out of trouble.

"Leave the pot."

"Huh? Oh, sure," he said, setting the pot of coffee on the table.

When he got back to Sue, he noticed that his palms were sweating.

"What'd she say?" Sue asked. "About what you'd expect," Rusty said.

"Pretty much nothing?" "Pretty much."

* * *

Rusty wants me to meet him at Mulga's Rush," Milla said to Drago.

They were parked a couple miles down Dunumbral Road. They didn't bother to try to hide their vehicles, since they figured by now all of Lightning Ridge knew who they were and that they were together. Their biggest fear at this point was that the locals wouldn't talk to them enough to share their secrets.

"We have to assume two things," Milla said. "One is that he thinks I'm working alone. The other is that he knows we're working together."

"We always work together," Mirko said. He was leaning out the driver's window, writing his name in the dirt with a long stick.

Drago, Milla, and Alek ignored him.

Drago said, "We'll head out early and be waiting for them. Make sure they give you what you want."

"No," Milla interrupted. "I'll go first. Rusty probably knows that place like the back of his hand and would notice if anything were out of place. You drive in behind me, give me 10 minutes to call. If you don't hear from me in 10 minutes, come get me."

"Drago, if you're driving in behind," Mirko said, "where will we be?"

"Dead if you don't shut your hole," Drago said calmly. "OK," Mirko said scratching his name in the dirt. "You

OK with that Alek?"

Alek didn't answer. Instead, he concentrated on his gun, lying disassembled, its parts spread out neatly on a white jeweler's cloth in the back seat of the car.

"If you're gone more than 10 minutes and they need some convincing to give up the goods, we'll roll in," Drago said.

"Guns blazing," Alek said. "Guns blazing," Mirko said.

* * *

Rusty and Sue were waiting at Mulga's Rush when Milla pulled up.

"Milla," Sue said pleasantly when Milla stepped out of Rusty's old ute.

"You didn't tell me she would be here," Milla said directly to Rusty, ignoring Sue.

"I figured it wouldn't hurt to have a witness," Rusty said.

"Where are they?" Milla asked.

"In your ute," Rusty said. He pointed to the ute Milla had given him. "Deal is you take the ute and the diamonds, give me back my ute, and take whatever, or whoever, you brought with you back to Sydney."

"And never come back," Sue said pleasantly. "I have to see them first."

"They're in the seat," Rusty said.

Rusty walked to the ute and pulled the latch to the driver's side door. He narrowed his eyes. Tried again. Locked.

"Door's locked," Rusty said. "Sue, did you lock the door?"

"I didn't want anybody to get the diamonds."

"Who is going to get the diamonds way out here?" Rusty spread his arms wide and turned a circle. "We're the only people for miles."

"I'm sorry," Sue said. "I don't know what I was thinking."

"Get the keys," Milla said calmly. "They're in the ute!" Rusty shouted. "You were supposed to take the diamonds and the ute! The keys are in the ute so you can take the ute!"

Milla glanced at her watch.

"Somewhere to be?" Sue asked.

"Not here," Milla said. "You have a hanger?"

Rusty moved his hands down his wrinkled clothes like a model highlighting a fashionable wardrobe. "Does it look like I own a hanger?"

"I'll look inside," Sue said.

"I'll look out back," Rusty said.

"If this is a set up," Milla said, "it is the worst set up in the history of set ups."

She leaned against the ute, checked her watch. Almost 10 minutes. *Why didn't I say fifteen? Everything takes longer out here.*

When Rusty returned, he was carrying a pickaxe. He raised it to the driver's side window.

"Woah, wait!" Milla cried out. "What are you doing?" "Getting the keys. There's enough diamonds in there to buy a thousand windows."

"Wait. Just wait," Milla said. "Let me help Sue find something to unlock the door."

Rusty looked like a lunatic with the pickaxe still raised high above his head. Milla made a wide path around him, electing to go around the passenger side of the ute, rather than take a chance on getting too close to Rusty.

Rusty realized how maniacal he must look and lowered the pickaxe as Milla rounded the corner of the ute.

"Holy dooley," Milla cried out. Rusty raised his pickaxe. "What?" Sue ran from the shack. "What is it?"

"Rusty, you're passenger window is out, you dipstick." Rusty lowered the pickaxe and felt his face redden. He had forgotten that one of the Serbs had busted it out the night before.

He glanced at Sue. Her face was red, too.

Milla unlocked the door, opened it, and pulled the small bag of diamonds from the ute.

She emptied the diamonds into her hand. "Four diamonds? Four diamonds?" She walked calmly around the back of the ute, her eyes fixed on Rusty. "You brought me out here for four diamonds?"

"They're beauts," Rusty said, backing up. He tripped on the pickaxe and immediately Milla was on top of him, pummeling him, swearing at him in a language he could not understand.

Sue ran toward them, pulled Milla from Rusty, and began striking Milla's perfectly maintained face with her strong, rough, server's hands. "Don't attack my boyfriend," Sue screamed over and over.

Rusty lifted himself to his feet and pulled Sue off Milla. He bent to help Milla, while holding Sue behind him with his backside. "Are you OK?" Rusty asked over Sue's screams.

She nodded, her blond hair, once perfect and clean and fragrant, now disheveled and dirty and odorous fell across her bloody and already bruising face.

He turned to Sue. "Calm down," he said. "It's done.

You're done."

He turned back to Milla, brushed her hair from her face, and asked again, "Are you OK?"

"I am," she said. "But I have to go. Now."

She and Rusty bent to pick up her diamonds from the ground. Their eyes met, locked momentarily. They smiled, then stood up close together, just in time for an explosion to send them flying through the air and to the ground.

* * *

Why do I always have to drive?" Mirko asked. "Alek always gets to set in the back. I always have to drive.

Why don't you drive? You're not doing anything." "Stop the car," Drago said.

Mirko continued to drive toward Mulga's Rush.

"Stop the car," Drago said. "I'll drive."

Mirko slammed on the brakes. The car stopped suddenly in the middle of the highway.

Drago glanced behind them. "Get out. I'll drive."

Mirko grabbed the two foot stick he had placed between the seat and the driver's side door, walked around to the passenger's side, and got in.

Drago slid over. "Now shut up," Drago said.

When they stopped, they lost sight of Milla's rusty old ute, but he had been over this country so much over the last couple of days that he knew where to go. As for giving Milla ten minutes to do her business, Drago just figured he'd give her a little extra time.

When they reached the long road leading out to Mulga's Rush, Drago pulled over to wait. He glanced in his rearview mirror at Alek, who was trying to load his gun with his sausage fingers. He looked over at Mirko. "What are you doing?" Drago asked.

"What's in that glove compartment, boss?" Mirko asked. "Gloves," Drago said.

"I never saw it opened before," Mirko said. "Why'd you never open it before?"

Drago ignored him and stared out the window. He tried to fight off the constant thoughts of inferiority that plagued him. He tried to fight off his fears that it would always be like this or, worse yet, that it would end like this. Not with a bang, but a whimper, he thought the line went. It had been so long since he had read anything worth reading that he had forgotten much of the meaningful things he had read. If the so many great things could be so easily forgotten, where did that leave him? Just here in this moment, as easily forgotten as the last moment?

"I guess," he said quietly to himself and shook his head. "Thanks, boss," Mirko said.

"Huh?" Drago said, turning in time to see Mirko push a tiny red button at the back of the glove compartment. "No!" Drago shouted, but he was too late.

A moment later, the car shook, and they saw a plume of smoke rise from the direction of Rusty's shack at Mulga's rush.

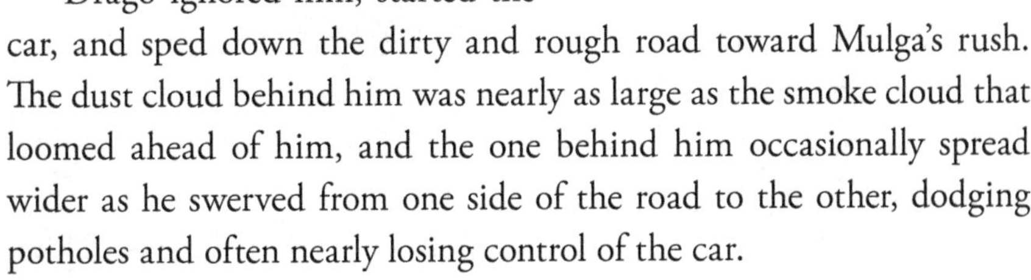

"Did I do that?" Mirko asked.

Drago ignored him, started the car, and sped down the dirty and rough road toward Mulga's rush. The dust cloud behind him was nearly as large as the smoke cloud that loomed ahead of him, and the one behind him occasionally spread wider as he swerved from one side of the road to the other, dodging potholes and often nearly losing control of the car.

When they pulled up to Rusty's property, Rusty was pulling Milla from the ground. The other girl was picking herself up. The other girl immediately ran to Rusty and began to alternate between beating on his chest with her fists and slapping his face with her open hands.

When Milla saw Drago's car, she picked up the pickaxe, raised it above her head, and ran toward the car.

"For a tiny thing, she sure is strong," Alek said.

Drago was unsure what to do—get out of the car and run or stay in the car and hope that it protected him from her fury.

Milla slammed the pickaxe into the windshield in front of Drago's face. It struck broadside, so the glass merely spider-webbed.

"What should we do?" Mirko asked.

Drago watched her raise the pickaxe above her head, stagger backwards, and strike the windshield again.

This time, the pick struck the windshield and burst through, striking the steering wheel. Milla struggled to pull it free, but it was wedged tightly into the hole it had made. "First the tracking device, and then you plant a bomb!

You tried to kill me," she shouted. "I'll kill you." "Mirko, shoot her," Drago said calmly.

Mirko turned to look at Alek. Alek shook his head subtly.

"Mirko, shoot," Drago said, less calmly.

Milla tried to work the pickaxe from the windshield. He glanced past her and could see Rusty and the other girl watching. Milla was making a fool of him. He pulled his own gun from the holster he kept beneath his shirt. He pointed the gun at her. From behind him, Alek's gun moved slowly into view.

"You do it, since the idiot won't," Drago said. He turned to Alek to find Alek's gun pointing at him, only inches from his nose.

"You better apologize to Milla," Alek said. "Apologize? Are you suddenly a gentleman?" "No," Alek said. "I always have been."

"Drago, give the gun to Mirko," Milla said through the windshield, "and get out of my car."

Drago looked at Mirko, then Alek, his gun still held close to him. Drago swung quickly toward Mirko and fired the gun, the shot striking Mirko directly in the chest.

Mirko raised his eyebrows, surprised, then looked down at his check, the blood already soaking his pressed, white, button-down shirt.

He calmly took the gun from Drago, emptied the clip, and dropped it to the floor.

Alek looked to Milla for guidance.

"Drago, get out of my car," Milla said calmly. "This is my car," Drago said.

"This was your car," Milla said and pulled open the door.

Drago reluctantly stepped out of the car.

Milla slid into the driver's seat and rolled down the window. "Walk," she said. "Where?"

"Out there," she said, pointing into the Outback. "How far?"

"Until you can't see anything."

Drago began to walk westward.

Milla pushed the gas slightly and followed him across the rough, nearly impassable landscape. The pickaxe eventually fell from the windshield, and through the broken glass, Milla could hear Drago whimpering. He walked slowly, tripping and glancing over his shoulder at her. She had not followed him far before the sun dropped quickly below horizon. Milla did not turn on the lights. When she could no longer see to drive, she stopped the car.

Without being asked, Alek stepped out of the car. Milla could not see what was happening in front of her, but she could hear the shuffle of feet across the ground, then the begging of a man who was too small for the trouble he made, and then the firing of a single shot, its exit from the chamber lighting the darkness for an instant.

Alek opened the passenger side door and pulled Mirko from the car, struggling to pull his partner's heavy body to its final resting place beneath the stars of the Outback. For an instant, Milla thought she heard Alek sobbing, but when he sat down in the passenger seat beside her, he seemed to be his usual, stoic self.

Milla sat staring into the darkness until she could not tell if her eyes were opened or closed. She fingered the four diamonds in her pocket and knew that even if she did not get exactly what she came looking for, she got more than what she had bargained for, and she would return to Sydney tomorrow a changed woman.

* * *

Immediately after the explosion, Rusty rushed to help Milla from the ground, forgetting for an instant that Sue was nearby when the explosion occurred. He forgot only for an instant, because in the next instant, Sue was pounding on him, slapping him, and screaming at him, like a woman gone mad.

From the corner of his eye, he saw a black Holden drive onto his property. Behind him, he heard Milla lift something from the ground and walk toward the car. He got hold of Sue's arms and turned her to watch what was occurring at the other side of his property.

Without speaking, they watched Milla strike the windshield with the pickaxe. Then they heard the muffled sound of a gunshot. Rusty half expected Milla to fall over dead, but instead, the driver, who Rusty now recognized as Drago, stepped from the car, and Milla slid into the driver's seat.

They watched as Drago walked slowly into the wilderness, the Holden following closely and slowly behind him.

"That car will never make it through there," Rusty said. But he continued to be surprised as the vehicle grew smaller and smaller and the darkness grew thicker and thicker both around it and around he and Sue, as the flames from the explosion finally run out of fuel.

"We're done, Rusty," Sue finally said. "We are, Sue," Rusty said.

In the distance, a single gunshot rang out, as if emphasizing the finality of their decision.

They sat down on the dirt together, watching the darkness for the return of the Holden. When the heat of the destroyed ute was no longer strong enough to keep them warm, Sue asked Rusty to take her home.

At her home, when she closed her front door without waving goodbye to him, Rusty wondered if this was good- bye for good. But for some reason, when he passed Milla driving slowly south on Castlereagh Highway, presumably back to Sydney, he knew that he and Sue would get past all of this craziness and find their own simple, comfortable craziness again.

CHAPTER 10

KATE LOOKS UP NIGEL SMITH

Three weeks had gone by since the Lightning Ridge Opal Festival. Kate picked up her cell phone and dialed the number given to her by Nigel Smith at the auction. "Yeah, this is Kate. I met you at the opal festival and told you I might have a couple of diamonds for sale." Kate listened to Nigel talking to her. "Yeah, say, I have to be in Melbourne on Thursday of next week to pick up a piece of mining equipment. If you are available, I'll bring in those two diamonds I have and let you take a look." Kate listened to what the man said. "Alright, I'll see you at 2:00 on Thursday at your place. I have the address you gave me on your card. Is that correct?" Kate listened. "Alright, hooroo. See you then." Kate hung up the phone. She had lied about having to pick up the mining equipment, but she didn't want to appear anxious that the only reason she was coming to Melbourne was to try and sell her two diamonds.

When Kate got to Melbourne around noon on Thursday she found the address to be one in an old building near the wharf. To kill some time, she went into a nearby deli and ordered a sausage roll and a cup of black coffee. She took her time eating her lunch while watching all the people pass by the deli walking up and down the wharf. A few minutes before 2:00, Kate made her way into the old building and up to the second floor. There she found the number on the door that matched the number on the card that Nigel had given her. It was an old building, and no name was on the door. Kate entered the dirty room with some old desks stacked with papers and a couple of old typewriters. The room wasn't that big. Nigel was sitting at a large, old wooden desk with his back to an open window with a broken pane. In a rather gruff voice, he greeted Kate.

In order to start the conversation, Kate said, "I didn't have any problem finding your place."

"Well, what did you bring to show me?" Nigel asked. Like Kate, this was a man of few words.

"I have a 4 carat and a 2 carat stone to show you."

"Are these some more stones from Allah's Rush?" asked Nigel.

"I'm not saying where they came from. Just that I have them, and they are for sale," Kate said sharply.

Nigel looked down at the diamonds, rolled them over in his fingers, picked up a jeweler's loop he had laying on his desk, and, not really responding to Kate, said, "Hummm." Then, to try to put Kate on the defense, he said, "I'm sure you know about the Kimberley process and all the paperwork involved with diamonds?"

"Yes, well these were a couple I found in a dry river bed up in Queensland. And, no, I don't have any paperwork with them."

"Interesting," Nigel responded flatly. "Well, what do you want for them?"

"Well, you paid eighteen and nineteen hundred dollars at the auction for similar 2 carat stones. How about eighteen hundred for the 2 carat stone and five thousand for the 4 carat stone."

Nigel chuckled at Kate's response. "I don't think they're worth that much, and, besides, you don't have any paperwork to back them up."

Kate, not to be out done, said, "Alright, if you're not interested, I'll be leaving." She abruptly swept the diamonds off the desk, turned around, and headed for the door.

"Well, now, wait a minute. I didn't say I wasn't interested. I'll give you a thousand dollars for the 2 carat stone and four thousand for the 4 carat stone. That's all I'm willing to pay. In the uncut diamond market and you not having any paper work, that's a very fair price."

Kate thought about it for a moment. Reflecting on the fact that she had nothing in the stones, she replied, "Well, alright. That's fine. I need the cash to pay for the mining equipment I came down here for."

Kate passed the stones back to Nigel who reached in the top drawer of his desk, opened a small metal box, and pealed out five thousand dollars in one hundred dollar bills. He handed them to Kate.

"If you find anymore diamonds up that river bed. Let me know. I might be interested."

"Fair dinkum. If I do, I got your number." With that, Kate left Nigel's office. As she went down the stairs of the old building, Kate grinned to herself. She was very happy with her sale.

CHAPTER 11

THE MELBOURNE BLACKMAIL

Boris, take a look at this." Nigel peered through a microscope at one of the diamonds he purchased from Kate. They both took turns looking through the microscope. "Alright now take a look at this diamond." Nigel removed the first diamond and placed a second, similar in size diamond under the microscope. "This is one of the two diamonds I purchased at the Lightning Ridge Opal Festival auction." Again both Boris and Nigel took turns peering into the microscope at the second diamond.

Boris turned to Nigel and said, "They both look the same!"

"I've been looking at diamonds for forty years. I tell you these diamonds all came out of the same location. By the color and trace marking of the stones, they are not from different locations. I was puzzled when that old crow told me she found them in a dry riverbed in Queensland. When I saw that ad in the *Sydney Morning Herald* and read the editorial about this miner Ben dying in a tunnel accident at the Allah's Rush mine, it just didn't make sense to me that this woman, Kate, found these diamonds in Queensland. In that editorial, it said that mine location was from a hole in the ground and that Kate and some other fellow by the name of Rusty were looking for opal when this fellow was killed. You know what I think? I think that old miner found a bunch of diamonds down that hole and those two killed him. I wonder how many more diamonds those two got out of that hole? And another thing, that bush woman has no idea what they are worth. She sold me that 4 carat stone for four thousand dollars. That stone, uncut, is easily worth twenty-five thousand dollars. Those two dingoes have no idea what they got!"

"Yeah, Nigel, I wonder how many more stones those two have?"

"I don't know, but we are going to find out. That Kate got real fidgety when I mentioned the Kimberley process. You know it's been five years since that mine accident. Those two dingoes have been laying low for five years waiting for that story about Ben the miner to go away. You know, Boris, those local people in Lightning Ridge spent a half million dollars wanting to dig for diamonds at Allah's Rush and came up empty. I'll bet if they found out those two hayseeds ended up with a handful of diamonds out of that hole, they would hang them both."

"What's your plan, Nigel?" "I think we can get the rest of those diamonds for nothing.

That woman doesn't want to have anything to do with the authorities or leaving any trail or conversation about those diamonds. I think I'll call her and see if I can buy a couple more diamonds from her, larger ones if possible. When we have a meeting, I'll want you there, unknown to her that I'll have someone else present. Then I'll spring it on her."

"What's that, Nigel?"

"Then I'll tell her either she gives us the rest of the diamonds, or we are going to the authorities. I know a bush woman like that wants nothing to do with authorities, including the tax people. Something tells me we may have our hands on a treasure here. We got her right where we want her."

Both Boris and Nigel laughed and went back looking at the diamonds, both the ones Nigel had purchased at the auction and the two he purchased from Kate.

* * *

The following day Nigel called Kate. "Hi, Kate. Nigel here. I really liked those two diamonds you sold me.

Have you got any more?"

Kate finally said, "Yeah, I have a couple more stones I could sell you."

"I hope they are big ones. I liked that 4 carat stone." "I'm not sure of the carat weight. But they are bigger than that 2 carat stone I sold you. I'll have to check." "Look, I'll tell you what. I have a friend in Dubbo who has an office on Gipps Street right off of Victoria Park. It's very easy to get to. Let's meet there next week on Friday at 2:00."

"Yeah, I know Dubbo," said Kate. "Let's meet in the park. I like the outdoors better. I'll find a bench under a tree. I'm sure you'll find me."

"I can do that. See you then."

They both hung up the phone.

"Well, Boris, I told you that woman had more diamonds."

The following week, Nigel and Boris were on Gipps Street. They parked their black, four door Jaguar XF across from Victoria Park. Both Nigel and Boris were big men, and they were dressed in black pants and black shirts.

They spotted Kate sitting on a bench under a Wattle Bottlebrush tree.

"Hi, Kate. I want you to meet my partner, Boris. We have been buying and selling diamonds together for years. Did you bring your stones?"

Kate looked over Boris, questioning in her mind why he was here. But he was here, and she couldn't do anything about it. Kate would have preferred that only Nigel be there. Out of her pocket, she pulled two stones. "Yeah, I weighed them. This one came in at 4.7 carats and the other one weighed in at 3.5 carats. In the sun, both stones looked magnificent."

Both Nigel and Boris kept their composure, although they were very excited, as they knew from years of at looking at diamonds that these were two special stones. Nigel brought out his jeweler's loop and studied both stones with great care.

"These look very similar to the other two stones you sold me. How much do you want for them?"

"I think five thousand each would be very fair," said Kate.

"No, no, the most I could give you would be three thousand each."

"They are worth a lot more," said Kate.

"I don't know how much you know about the uncut diamond market here in Australia, but you will find very few in the whole country who will even talk to you about undocumented stones. I mentioned to you the Kimberley Process. The authorities are very serious about the movement of uncut diamonds in, out, and all around the country. I wasn't surprised to see those two Serbs at the Lightning Ridge auction. They are a couple of our competitors in the diamond market. Boris and I know this market better than anyone, and we are willing to take chances on undocumented stones."

Kate was getting nervous with all the speech-making by Nigel. "Well, how about four thousand each?"

"Kate, I'll tell you what, I came to Dubbo to buy stones from you.

I'll give you three thousand five hundred for each of them. That's my final offer."

"Alright, let's do it. Here are the stones. Give me your money."

Nigel pulled out a wad of bills from his pocket and handed Kate seven thousand dollars in hundred dollar bills.

"Well, Kate, have you got any more stones?"

Kate rolled her eyes at Nigel and Boris, still trying to size up Boris as he only watched and said nothing through the whole transaction. "I might have a few more."

"Well, I'll tell you, Kate, why don't you just give us the rest of the stones you have?"

"What are you saying? You want to buy them from me?"

Very calmly and in a low tone Nigel said, "No, I said I think you should give them to me."

Kate puffed up and looked very agitated. "Are you nuts!

You must have a screw loose in that coconut of yours!" "Kate, I know diamonds backwards and forwards. We looked at the stones you sold me under a microscope, as well as the two stones I purchase at the auction in Lightning Ridge. All these stones, including the auction stones, have the same color and trace markings. Any diamond expert can tell they all came from the same source. I think you and that Rusty fellow mentioned in the news article in the

Sydney Morning Herald stole those diamonds from that Ben fellow they found down that Allah's Rush hole and killed him. Your biggest mistake was selling me any diamonds, since I purchased two stones at that auction. Thus, I could make the comparison."

Kate stood there in shock, unable to speak for quite a while. Finally she said, "You can't prove a thing."

"No Kate, we got you dead to rights. You didn't get those stones out of a dry riverbed. There is no doubt they came from Allah's Rush. Now won't it be nice when all the Lightning Ridge people hear our story? If you're lucky, they'll just take you and that fellow Rusty out to Allah's Rush and throw you down that eighty foot hole you said you drilled looking for opal. I'll tell you what, I'll give you a couple of weeks to think it over. You know we're right. It's no wonder you waited these five, long years before trying to sell these diamonds. Just waiting for time to let people forget. You didn't plan on that editor at the *Sydney Morning Herald* reprinting that story."

Kate said nothing.

"Nice doing business with you. Give me a call, and we'll get together for the rest of the diamonds."

Nigel and Boris turned around and headed for their car. Kate sat down on the bench under the tree, trying to figure out her next move. For the first time she felt trapped.

CHAPTER 12

THE WAR AHEAD

Kate, all her life, defended herself, whether it be from ratters or from wild animals. The time she killed the wild cat that was attacking young calves in the bush she had by her side her Smith & Wesson M657 revolver, her 30-30-lever action Winchester rifle model 94, and her Winchester model 1300, 12-gauge pump shotgun. She was ready for war and was not about to back down from anyone. If the Russians and the Serbs wanted a war, Kate was ready.

* * *

The two week warning that Nigel had given Kate had gone by. Kate called Nigel. "Alright Nigel, you win. Come and collect the diamonds. Rusty and I are working my sheep, but if you come up next Thursday, I'll give you the diamonds. Let's make it at 8:00 P.M. at The Club in the Scrub. That's a pub out here southwest of Lightning Ridge near Cumborah. I'll give the directions on how to get here. It's not difficult." Kate gave Nigel additional driving directions off road to the pub. Kate made it short. "Alright, see you then."

When they got off the phone, Boris was with Nigel in his office.

Nigel laughed. "Well, Boris, I told you that old crow would cough. Tell Victor and Alex we want them to follow us up in a second car next Thursday to Lightning Ridge. We'll give her a show of force that we mean business."

They both laughed.

* * *

Jasper Jones was tending the bar at The Pub in the Scrub.

Kate said to Jasper, "I'm going to have a private party here next Thursday staring at 8:00 P.M., so I need you to clear everyone out by then. I'll pay you five hundred dollars for that evening. If anything gets destroyed, I'll pay you for that too. Any beer we drink, you can bill me for, also. I don't think you want to be around that night. I'll lock the place up and get with you the next day and settle up. It's probably going to get pretty rough. Rusty and I have some guys coming from Melbourne who think we have a bunch of opal, and they want to blackmail us for it. Dirty ratters! I got some of the fellows to come in and make sure nothing gets out of control. We're going to let these fellows know they can't come out here in the bush and push us around. So, Jasper, just stay out of the way."

"Not a problem, Kate. I remember how you took care of Bruce years ago down Rusty's mine. It's all yours Kate. Go get 'em! Leave me out of the way!"

"Unfortunately, we have to teach these city boys a lesson, or they will want to move in and control everything up here."

* * *

On Thursday, Kate arranged for a couple of the local sharp shooters to be outside in the dark once the Russians were inside. She knew it wouldn't take much to scare them off, coming out of the bar into the darkness. Carl positioned himself behind a tree with a good view of the door of the pub. Ralph, one of the best shots in the area, hid behind a rock. Kate had instructed both of them to not kill anyone, just give them enough notice not to stay around.

When the Russians pulled up in front of the pub, it was just at twilight and visibility was excellent. Nigel had no problem with Kate's directions to the pub with Victor and Alex following in a separate car behind Nigel. All four got out of their cars, looked around the area, and entered the door at the front of the pub. The lights were on in the pub. Part of the sitting area was darker than the lights behind the bar. Kate and Rusty had positioned themselves at one of tables in the rear. Kate's Smith & Wesson M657 revolver was lying on the table. Rusty had a rifle also at a position, leaning against a chair by his side, but not visible to anyone entering the pub. Kate had already locked the back door of the pub so that the only entrance or exit was through the front door.

"Hi, boys," said Kate. "Welcome to The Club in the Scrub. This is one of the local watering holes for us around here. Rusty, get these boys a beer. I'm sure you're dry from your drive. Unfortunately, we don't have any VB. All we have is Tooheys."

Rusty got up from his chair and walked behind the bar and started filling schooners from the Tooheys pump. All the fellows picked up a schooner and sat down at two of the tables. Rusty drew himself a schooner of beer and went back to the table he was sitting at.

Nigel opened the conversation. "Where are all the local folks?"

"Oh, I thought we should have a private party. I sent them on their way for the night. There are other pubs nearby, so no one will miss a drink this night," said Kate evenly.

All sat there for several minutes, enjoying the moment and their glass of beer.

"Thanks for the beer, Kate, but where are the diamonds?" asked Nigel.

"Well, fellows, here is your answer. There are no more diamonds. This is opal country. You'll never convince anyone that there are diamonds around here." Kate spoke low and carefully. "What you fellows need to know is this area doesn't like ratters. I have let it be known that we are having this meeting tonight with a bunch of blackmailing opal ratters. While a lot of us run sheep and cattle in this area, most of us are opal miners. Over the years, we have been plagued by ratters. We hate ratters. What you fellows need to know is this pub is surrounded by a lot of my fellow opal miners who don't take kindly to outsiders. Now, fellows, you best be calm, if you want to get out of here alive."

Boris turned to Nigel in amazement and said, "Nigel, what did you get us into?"

Nigel looked at Kate and gritted his teeth. "You dirty bitch. You're not going to get away with this!"

"Nigel, be calm if you want to get out of here alive. You and your boys are not in Melbourne. This is bush country, and we are in control. Don't think you can come out here and push us around. This is our territory," said Kate calmly. "I think you best leave now, and don't trip going out the door. I hope you all get to your cars and down the road," said Kate with a slight grin.

Nigel motioned to Victor and Alex to go out the door first with Boris close behind. All the Russians were carrying handguns, and they had them drawn, as they went out the door of the pub. It was dark with the light from the pub behind them; thus, they were blinded trying to look off in the darkness. All of a sudden a shot rang out, and Victor, the first out the door, was hit in the left leg.

Victor cursed and whirled,

looking for who shot him. It was dark. He was blinded. He headed for the car as fast as he could go. Suddenly, a second shot was heard breaking glass in the back window of the car Victor was heading for. Another shot rang out, and Alex was shot in his right shoulder. Another shot broke more car glass. This time it was a side window of Nigel's Jaguar XF. Boris and Nigel made it to their car without incident. Both cars were quickly started and spun gravel, as they left the pub.

"Nigel, do you remember how to get out of this place? It was light when we got here! Now it's dark and all this dust!"

"Oh, shut up, Boris! Let me figure this out!"

Nigel kicked up such a cloud of dust in the dark that he was having a hard time trying to figure out where to turn, and he slowed down. As he did so, the car behind him in which Victor and Alex were riding banged into the back of Nigel's Jaguar XF. Nigel swore but kept on driving.

CHAPTER 13

KATE'S WILD BOAR HUNT

Kate called Dutch. "Yeah, hi, Dutch. I got a problem, and I need your help."

"Anything, Kate. You know I'm always ready to give you a hand. Are we loading sheep?"

"Nah, nothing like that. You'll like this one. I got three pesky wild boars that keep coming around, tearing up my grain feeders and driving my dogs crazy. There doesn't seem to be a litter of pigs, just these three big old boars hanging out together. I've had it with them. We can use my dogs. I'll need you and your Quad."

"Oh, what great fun! I haven't been on a pig hunt for a long time!" said Dutch.

"Well, look, we're going to need Rusty and his Quad. I haven't talked to him yet. It will take all three of us and my dogs to run down those varmints. Sam Waters has a lot of hunting gear. I'll go see him. Maybe he'll lone me a couple of dog cages and dog collars. You know one dog collar, new, costs one hundred and fifty dollars. I only want to get these three boars. I'm not interested in hunting hogs for sport. Sam's boys are always out on the weekend. For young fellows, that is one of the best sports here in the bush."

"Okay Kate, let me know when you want to go. I'm not doing much and not mining opal right now. I don't have a shearing job at the moment. I've been waiting for the boys to call me at the Dubbo sales yard."

"Take care. I'll let you know when I get everything organized. Hooroo for now." Kate hung up her phone.

* * *

Hi, Sam. It's Kate. I need something from you. I wonder if you could help."

"Sure, Kate. What is it?" questioned Sam.

"I got these three hogs driving me crazy. They're tearing up my feed troughs and driving my dogs crazy."

"I'll send the boys over, and we'll get them for you." "No, Sam. I would rather do if myself. I know pretty much where this gang hangs out. I've already got Dutch and Rusty to help me. I got my three dogs. As you know, if you get too many dogs and people involved, someone might get shot, or a dog gets torn up. If any dogs get hurt, I would rather they be mine."

"Alright, Kate, what is it then you want from me?" "Sam, you would do me a big favor if you would loan me a couple of your dog cages and three of your dog collars. You know those collars cost at least one hundred and fifty dollars. I don't want to buy any. If I damage any of your equipment, you know I'll make it good."

"Yeah, Kate, you can have the equipment. I sure hate to have the boys miss a good fight, but it's your gig. When do you want the equipment?"

"I'll come out and pick it up at your place. When is a good time for you?"

"Let's make it tomorrow about noon. I'll be up from the mine for lunch. I'm not finding much in the mine these days. Just picking around looking for some place to go. See you at noon."

"Thanks, Sam." Kate hung up the phone.

* * *

Hey, Rusty. Want to have some fun?"

"Kate, I thought you were all business. I never heard of you ever wanting to have fun."

"Well, those wild hogs are driving me crazy. I got Sam Waters to loan me a couple of dog cages and three dog collars. I don't want to spend the money for something I'll never use again. Rusty, can you help? I got Dutch standing by, and he said he could load up his Quad and bring it with him. If you bring yours then we have my three dogs, and we'll have three Quads to chase those buggers down."

"Alright, Kate. I haven't been on a pig hunt for a long time. It should be fun. I've got a big knife to slit their throat. We'll get those critters. Just let me know when you want to do it."

"I've got to pick up Sam Water's equipment tomorrow at noon. I'll call you in a couple of days when we can start. I know where those hogs hang out. You know they tend to be rather territorial. There only seems to be three big boars. I don't know why. I haven't seen any female or litter of pigs. Maybe that's why there are three males running together. I'll catch you later." Kate hung up the phone.

* * *

Two days later, Kate called Rusty. "How about tomorrow at 10:00 to hunt hogs?" Kate listened to Rusty on the other end of the phone. "Alright, see you then."

In like manner, she called Dutch, who also said he could show up at 10:00 in the morning.

"Alright fellows," said Kate. "Let's fit up two of these dogs with Sam Water's collars, put them in a cage on the back of my Quad. We'll do the same with the other dog and put him on your Quad, Rusty. Let's take our rifles. I got my Smith & Wesson M657 revolver, but I don't plan to shoot anybody."

Dutch thought that was funny and let out a big laugh.

"You better take a bottle of water. I'm bringing a big thermos of coffee if someone wants a drink. I also have a five pound sack of corn and chickpeas, in case we need to draw out those hogs in the bush somewhere. Alright fellows, I think we got everything. Let's go."

Both Rusty and Dutch followed Kate's lead off in the bush, keeping a safe distance from running into each other. Kate was out about a mile, drove down in a small ravine, and all of sudden spotted one of the boars. The dogs started to bark, having picked up its scent.

Kate raised her hand, indicating all to stop. "Alright, fellows, let's turn the dogs loose and let them do their job." Kate quickly opened the cage on her Quad. Dutch beat Rusty to releasing the single dog in the cage behind Rusty. The three of them got back on their Quads and followed the dogs. The dogs were fresh and shortly cornered the boar. All three hunters jumped from their Quads and sprang toward the malaise of squealing hog and barking dogs, tearing at the boar. Kate got a hold of two of her dogs, and Dutch grabbed the third, while Rusty was already at the throat of the boar and quickly dispensing it with his twelve inch Bowie knife.

Kate was elated. "Well fellows that went well. You would think we were professional hog wranglers! I hope we get the other two that quickly. Dutch, hook the hog to the back of the Quad and drag him out to the road for show."

"Fair dinkum, Kate."

Unfortunately, no one in this area will eat wild hog. Just about all of them are full of worms and not considered fit for human consumption. However, it is the custom to line the kill along the road as a trophy. It has always been done that way. If not, they would have left it in the bush to be consumed by other wild animals including hawks and vultures. Even placing it along the road, the carcass would be consumed within a couple of days. Nothing goes to waste in the bush.

"It's about 11:30, and with this clear sky and no breeze, it's getting hot. I would guess it's close to one hundred degrees Fahrenheit." Kate's dogs were back in their cages. She poured the remaining water in her bottle over her three dogs. "It's been a good morning. Let's get these dogs back to my place and some shade and water. I don't want them to get heat stroke."

All three drove back to Kate's cabin and Dutch dropped off the dead boar by the side of the road as was the custom. "I'll tell you what boys. Let's go get a couple of beers at The Club in the Scrub. My treat. Tomorrow, I think we should start out at 9:00 to get our second boar. I just don't want to overheat these dogs."

"Right on, Kate. I'm always ready for a beer. Let's celebrate!" said Dutch.

With Dutch's last remark, they all jumped in their utes and headed for The Club in the Scrub. As they entered the pub, Kate saw Carl and Ralph at one of the tables having a beer. These were the two sharp shooters who hid outside and helped Kate the night the Russians showed up from Melbourne.

"Hi, gents," said Kate. "Can we join you at your table? We're here to celebrate a boar kill, but I also owe you two fellows a couple of beers for helping me the night the Russians showed up. Jasper, beer all around!"

"So Kate, what's this about a boar hunt?" asked Carl.

"Well, fellows, I've had it with those three big boars tearing up my feed troughs for quite a while. I finally decided I'd had enough. Dutch and Rusty are helping me locate them. We got one today. It's so hot out there that's all my dogs can take. We're going to try again tomorrow to see if we can corner a second hog."

Ralph raised his glass of beer and the others followed.

"Good luck, Kate. Those hogs are really hard to catch." "We'll get them. I've had it with those three."

* * *

The next day, they again gathered at Kate's cabin and loaded the dogs into the metal cages on the back of Kate and Rusty's Quads. They drove back to the same location where they caught the boar the day before. They spent at least an hour circling the area and coming up with no sightings of the boars.

Kate waved and all stopped. "Fellows, let's take a look about a mile east of here where the bore drain runs through the edge of my property. Maybe we'll find them there. That's a good place where all the animals in the area get their water."

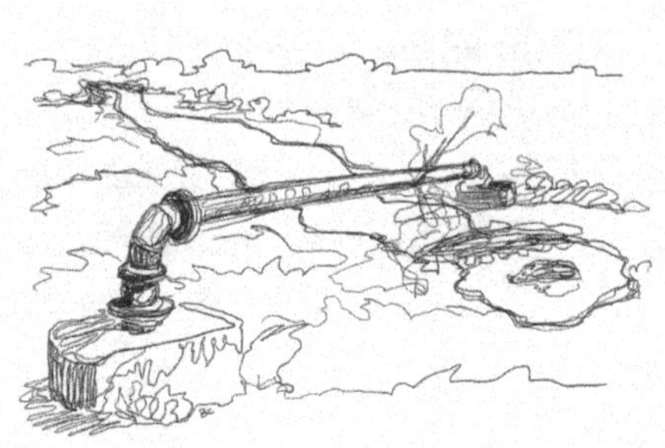

When they reached the bore drain and drove down along the ridge of the drain, they sighted an area with a big pig wallow. It appeared the hogs had rooted a hole in the bore drain, creating a mud hole where the pigs cooled off at night.

"Look at that wallow. Those hogs have been here lately."

About that time, the dogs picked up the scent of the hogs and started barking. Kate looked around, trying to see the boars.

"Okay, fellows, let's turn the dogs loose," said Kate. The dogs took off with all three on their Quads in pursuit.

It wasn't long before the dogs had a second hog cornered, and they were biting on its ears and tail. Kate, Rusty, and Dutch quickly grabbed the dogs, and Rusty brought out his Bowie knife and dispensed the hog. Suddenly out of the bush came the third hog, running towards them.

It was enormous. It had huge tusks, and they could tell it had to weigh at least two hundred pounds. This was one of the largest boars any of them had ever seen.

"Look out!" yelled Rusty, as he ducked behind his Quad.

The boar ran between Kate and Dutch with one tusk catching Dutch's pants and ripping a hole in the lower portion of his bib overalls. Fortunately for Dutch, the boar's tusk did not damage his leg. The hog was screaming as he passed and ran into the near bush and disappeared.

"Man! That was a close one!" exclaimed Dutch.

All three were shaken by the experience. Once they got their composure, they gathered up the three dogs, which were not injured by the bedlam created when the boar passed through. Fortunate for the dogs, they were leashed and held by Kate and Dutch before the boar appeared. Had they not been leashed, the dogs would have pounced on the enormous boar, and there would have been several severe injuries. The dogs were put back in their cages, and again Dutch hooked up the dead boar to drag it back to the road as a trophy.

"There is no question we are done for the day," said Kate. "But I'll tell you what, we are done chasing hogs. I'm going to get in touch with Sam Waters again and ask if we can borrow that big steel hog trap he has. This animal is too dangerous to set our dogs on that boar. I think he is the ringleader for this gang of three. I've got to get him, but I'm not willing to risk injury or death to my dogs or injury to us."

When they returned to Kate's cabin, she called Sam Waters. "Sam, we got two out of three of those pesky boars. We got one to go, and he is a big fellow. Huge tusks and looks to weigh over two hundred pounds.

He's a smart one too. Just as we killed our second boar, he ran out of the bush straight into Dutch, Rusty, and the dogs as we were loading up. He is an animal not to mess with." Kate listened to Sam talking. "No, Sam, I don't want your boys to hunt him. He is too dangerous, and I don't want anyone or our dogs to get hurt. I know where he will be. We found a pig wallow down along one of the bore drains on the edge of my property. Sam, what I would like is for Dutch to drive over to your place tomorrow and pick up that huge metal cage you have for catching hogs. I'll bait it with some corn and chickpeas. I'm positive we'll get him that way. Those hogs love corn and chickpeas." Kate again listened to Sam. "No, Sam, just loan me the cage. I don't want to complicate this kill."

Again, Kate listened to Sam. "Thanks, Sam. Dutch will be over about 11:00 tomorrow to pick up the cage." Kate hung up the phone.

"Is that alright with you, Dutch? To pick up the cage from Sam's and bring it back here?" asked Kate.

"Not a problem, Kate," said Dutch.

"Rusty, I think Dutch and I can set up that cage down at the pig wallow. We don't need three of us to do this, and there's no dogs involved," said Kate.

"Alright, Kate. If you need me just let me know." "Rusty, I always appreciate your help. You too, Dutch.

Two of us can handle that cage," said Kate.

"I don't know about you, fellows, but I'm still a little shook up with that boar attacking us. We're done for today. But I owe you both some more beers at the pub."

Dutch, not to miss the moment, said, "Right on Kate. I'll drink to that."

They all laughed and parted their ways.

* * *

The following day as Kate had requested, Dutch picked up the metal cage from Sam Watters place and was back at Kate's cabin by 2:00 P.M.

"Sam helped me load the cage. This is a big one. I think it's strong enough to hold that big boar. Sam showed me how to set the door and lock. It's definitely a two person job moving this thing," said Dutch.

"Well, you and the cage are here. Do you mind if we set it up this afternoon?" asked Kate.

"That's what I'm here for. It's not that rough getting down to that bore drain where the pig wallow is. We'll leave it on my ute and drive it there."

"Great, Dutch. Before we go, let's have a fresh cup of coffee, and I have a couple of fresh sausage rolls, which I know you will like," said Kate.

"Perfect, Kate. You know I love to eat."

They sat outside of Kate's cabin, eating sausage rolls, drinking coffee, and enjoying the calls of a kookaburra in a nearby eucalyptus tree and a flock of galahs landing in the field nearby, making noise.

It didn't take them very long to reach the location near the bore drain and the pig wallow. They unloaded the metal cage and set the door, and Kate got her five pound bag of corn and chickpeas she had carried with on the previous day's hunt. She poured the contents on the ground on the inside of the cage in the far end such that the boar could not reach the grain without entering the cage. In addition, Sam Waters instructed Dutch to stake down the corners of the metal cage, as it had been his experience that an old boar like Kate was trying to catch would merely push the cage aside to get to the grain.

"Gee, Dutch, I'm glad you talked to Sam. I would never have thought about staking this cage. Smart move!" said Kate.

"Dutch, let's get down here early tomorrow to see if we got this fellow. I don't want that boar to stay in that cage so long that he figures out how to get out of it. How about showing up at 7:00, and we'll check out the cage?"

"I'll be here."

"Oh, and, Dutch, when we are done, my treat for breakfast at the Blue Light Café."

"Right on, Kate."

* * *

The next day, Dutch was at Kate's right at 7:00, and this time they rode out in Kate's ute. She had her Smith & Wesson M657 revolver and her 30-30-lever action Winchester rifle with her should they need to dispense the boar.

As they neared the metal cage, sure enough they saw they had caught this massive animal. When they got out of

Kate's ute, the boar was screaming and moving around shaking the metal cage. Two of the corner stakes had come loose. Kate wasted no time. She pulled out her revolver and shot two bullets into the boar's head. He was dead.

"Boy, Kate, you sure called this one right. What a massive animal. I can't remember when I've seen one this big. And look at the tusks on this fellow!"

"Dutch, I think he is so heavy, I'll have to back the ute up to the cage and, with this rope, pull him from the cage. Then we can load the cage."

"I agree."

As Kate's ute pulled on the boar, it remained stuck in the cage, which turned at an angle. They had to re-stake the cage and pull a second time. Once the dead boar was out, Dutch and Kate loaded the metal cage onto Kate's ute. As they pulled the boar back to Kate's cabin and along the artesian drain, two emu crossed in front of Kate's ute, moving very fast off into the bush.

Kate's dogs were at the cabin but were not tied up. When they smelled the dead boar, the dogs starting attacking the carcass, biting different parts of the animal and continually barking at it.

"Get back you pesky varmints!" Kate yelled at her dogs.

At the cabin, Dutch said, "I'll tie the boar to my ute and pull him out to the road."

"Thanks, Dutch. You might help me put the two dog cages I borrowed from Sam Waters on my ute. After I treat you to a big breakfast at the Blue Light Café in town, I'll take all this gear back to Sam's place. I'll see you at the café in a tick."

"Right on, Kate."

"Stay here," Kate commanded her dogs, as Dutch drove off with the dead boar in tow.

Kate finished loading the three dog collars she had borrowed from Sam.

* * *

Both Dutch and Kate ate a hearty breakfast that morning. It was about 9:30 and Kate put in a call to Sam Waters. "Sam! Guess what? We got our third boar. Let me tell you that metal cage of yours was the right way to go. Had we tried to surround him in the usual way with the dogs, there would have been a lot of injuries." Kate listened to Sam talking. "Say, Sam, I have all of your gear loaded up on my ute. Would you mind if I bring it out to your place now?" Kate listened to Sam talking. "Great Sam! I should be out there in about half-an-hour to forty-five minutes. See you then." Kate hung up the phone.

At Sam's camp, both Kate and Sam unloaded Sam's gear.

"What do I owe you, Sam? I don't think any of the collars or cages have been damaged. Even that big metal cage we used to catch that last monster looks okay."

"No, Kate, you owe me nothing. I was glad to do it. Sorry my boys didn't get in on all the excitement. If I need help sometime, I'll give you a call. Particularly with ratters."

Both Kate and Sam knew that Sam was referring not only the incident with the Russians but also to what had happened five years earlier with Bruce down Rusty's mine hole.

"Thanks again, Sam." Kate drove off in her ute.

CHAPTER 14

THE AMERICANS!

"Rusty, I'm at a dead end as to how we get rid of the rest of our diamonds. I don't want to go back to either those fellows in Melbourne or in Sydney. That whole idea of the diamond auction at the opal festival turned out to be a disaster."

"I've got one other idea," said Rusty. "I still have the phone number for Jack Cline in America. Why don't I try and get in touch with him and see if he would buy our diamonds?"

"Rusty, that was over five years ago, and we really did a number on him, and he knew it. I don't think that's even a long shot. I doubt your phone number is any good, and he probably won't even talk to you."

"Well, Kate, I can at least try," said Rusty.

"Do as you like. I think you're chasing a really fast kangaroo on this one."

Given the time difference between Australia and the United States, Rusty timed his phone call so that it was 10:00

A.M. in Los Angeles. The phone rang four times. Rusty was about to hang up when he heard a man's voice on the other end say, "Hello?"

"Is this Jack Cline?" "Yes, who is this?"

"It's Rusty in Lightning Ridge, Australia."

"Good lord! It's been over five years since I last talked to you. What do you want? I'm done investing in opals or Australian opal mines. So, Rusty, go chase someone else!" Jack was ready to hang up the phone.

"Wait a minute, Jack. At least let me tell you why I called," begged Rusty.

"Alright, make it quick. I've got a meeting to go to. It's your nickel, so talk. Make it fast," said Jack, rather exasperated that he was even listening to Rusty talk after all that he had gone through trying to finance Rusty's opal mine.

"Please don't hang up until you hear my whole story. I promise to make it short."

"Alright, Rusty, but it better be a good one. You and Kate really did me in on those opals."

"Okay, I understand. Well, the short of it is that Kate and I found some diamonds that were dug up in kimberlite we found below the opal level over eighty feet down. We've experienced some difficulty in trying to sell them in Australia and wondered if you or maybe one of your contacts would have an interest in purchasing them?"

"Well, that is a different story. Look, Rusty I'm not into buying or selling gemstones. When you and I met, I was only interested in raw opal for my cutting hobby. Nice story, though. I hope your find a buyer," Jack said, ready to hang up his phone.

"Wait! Wait! If you aren't interested, can you at least point me to someone who might be?"

"Well, I'll tell you what. I'll call my friend in Laguna Beach who is a jeweler I've been trading with for years. He might have a lead. That's the best I can do for you. I've got to ring off now. If my contact has an idea, I'll give you a call back. This number? It might be several days," said Jack.

"No worries, mate! Thanks for taking my call. I'll wait to hear from you."

"Yeah, yeah, I'll see what I can do." With that last exchange, Jack hung up the phone.

* * *

Jack had one of his business acquiesces sitting across his desk when Rusty called.

"That was a strange phone call," said the man.

"Yeah, those Aussies! They're a great bunch. Some of the funniest and most interesting people I've ever met. I've been to Australia many times. I've enjoyed every trip. However, about six years ago, I let myself be talked into investing in an opal mine in Lightning Ridge. One of the biggest mistakes I ever made. This fellow who just called and his lady friend did a number on me. I can't believe he even called me. Enough of this nonsense. Let's get back to business."

* * *

A couple days later, Jack gave his friend, Ned Wells, a jeweler from Laguna Beach, California a phone call.

"Hi, Ned. Say, I got a crazy call from that fellow from Australia. If you remember, I invested in his opal mine." Jack listened to Ned laughing.

"Yeah, yeah, I'm a sucker. Anyway, I listened to his new story this time. He claims that he and his lady found some diamonds in some kimberlite they hit below the Cretaceous about eighty feet down." Jack listened to Ned talk.

"Well, it sounded like a good story." More laugher by

Ned.

"Look, that fellow asked me if I knew anyone who might be interesting in buying their diamonds." Jack listens to more laugher.

"Alright, can you come up with a couple of contacts for the fellow? I am sure someone we met at the Tucson Gem Show might be interested." Jack hung up the phone.

* * *

Two days later Jack got a call from Ned. "Hi, Ned. What's new?"

"Well, Jack, I did find a couple of names you can give to that fellow in Australia. I called them both and told them your story and asked if I could give out their contact information. They said they didn't have a problem with that, as they were always looking for unusual gemstones. Both of these fellows buy and sell gems from all over the world. You don't know them, but I have talked with them both at the Tucson show. The first fellow is Charlie Keuper. He told me he gets to Sydney a lot, so that should turn into an easy meeting. The second fellow is Peter Grant. Grant didn't indicate anything about his travels looking for stones."

Ned went on and gave Jack all the contact information, which he could pass on to Rusty, and then they both hung up the phone.

* * *

A week later, Jack made contact with Rusty. "Hi, Rusty. I did what you asked. I got you information from a reliable source on two individuals in the gem trade that buy and sell gemstone all over the world. Look, I know nothing about them. It's up to you to get in touch with them. The first fellow's name is Charlie Keuper. I understand he goes to Sydney quite often. The second fellow is Peter Grant." Jack gave Rusty phone numbers where these two men could be contacted. "Good luck. This is the best I can do for you," said Jack.

Before signing off, Rusty responded, "Many thanks Jack. I am very sorry our opal mining deal didn't work out. I haven't found much since we spoke five years ago. I greatly appreciate this information."

"Yeah, whatever. Good luck." Jack hung up the phone.

CHAPTER 15

MEETING CHARLIE KEUPER IN SYDNEY

"Hi, Mr. Keuper. My name is Rusty. I'm from Lightning Ridge, Australia. I was told to contact you regarding some uncut diamonds my mate and I found here in Australia."

Charlie responded in a friendly voice, "That's a rather strange place to be finding diamonds. I know they find them in Queensland, and there are a lot of commercial diamonds mined in Western Australia. But in your area?"

"Well, it's a long story, but I wonder if my mate and I could meet with you sometime and show you what we have."

"I go all over the world looking at gemstones. I can meet with you, but it will have to be in Sydney. As a matter of fact, I'll be there for a gem and jewelry show next weekend. There is a show in the ballroom of the Four Seasons Hotel on George Street. I will be flying in from the U.S. just for that show. Look, you have my cell phone number should we miss each other. But let's try to meet in the hotel lobby at 2:00 P.M.

on Friday. I am a fellow, fifty years old with sand-yellow hair. I don't think you can miss me." With that description, Charlie laughed.

"Thanks. My mate and I will be there. Her name is Kate, and we have done a lot of business together here in Lightning Ridge."

"Well, I look forward to hearing your story and seeing your diamonds. I buy and sell all kinds of gemstones, but I always love to look at diamonds." With that last remark, Charlie hung up the phone.

* * *

Kate! You won't believe it. I got in touch with one of those Americans. His name is Charlie Keuper, and he is willing to meet us next Friday in Sydney."

"Are you sure he'll be there?" Kate scowled at Rusty over the phone.

"Look, Kate. What have we got to lose? Another trip to Sydney. We haven't had much luck with the Russians or the Serbs. We might as well give the Americans a shot."

"Alright, Rusty. I sure would love to be done with these diamonds. They have been nothing but trouble. Maybe this is the answer. Since you haven't had enough money to buy a new ute, I guess it's up to me to drive us down there."

"Kate, you know I am always available to help you with your sheep or cattle."

"Yeah, Rusty, don't you worry. I'll take it out of your hide!"

* * *

Kate and Rusty left early on the following Thursday from Lightning Ridge to get them down to Sydney off George Street on Friday morning. Kate found her same parking lot. They were there again by 10:00 A.M. The hotel was within a couple blocks from where they had parked.

Kate and Rusty brought with them all the remaining diamonds.

Charlie was sitting in a chair in the lobby of the hotel, reading the day's Wall Street Journal when Rusty and Kate promptly appeared at

2:00 P.M. They had no problem spotting Charlie, since there were few people in the lobby.

"Mr. Keuper?" inquired Rusty.

"Oh, yes," Charlie said as he looked up at Rusty and folded the newspaper he was reading.

"Mr. Keuper, this is Kate, the lady I mentioned. We work together on lots of things in Lightning Ridge. Mining opals, running sheep, and chasing cows."

They all laughed. "Look folks, let's go to my room on the tenth floor. I have a suite up there with a table. We don't want to talk business out here in the lobby," said Charlie.

"Sounds good to me," said Kate.

Once inside Charlie's room, they all sat down around a table with a view overlooking Sydney Harbor.

"Wow! Great view of the harbor," said Rusty.

"Yes it is. I've been to Sydney so many times I don't pay much attention to it anymore. It really is spectacular. Well, let's see what you folks have brought me," said Charlie.

Kate and Rusty both reached into their pockets and pulled out their dirty brown bags that contained the remaining diamonds they had not sold and poured them into two separate piles on the table. The light was just right coming from the window of Charlie's suite, giving each diamond a spectacular reflection in the sunlight.

Charlie looked at the two separate piles, not showing much emotion, but clearly stunned. He looked at the diamonds and then looked at Rusty and Kate. "You two really don't know what you have here?" questioned Charlie. Kate wanted to control the conversation and didn't want to give too much away. "Well, Mr. Keuper," Kate said a little too loudly. She was quickly interrupted by Charlie. "Just call me Charlie. Everyone does. I'm not keen on that Mr. stuff."

Both Rusty and Kate felt more relaxed by Charlie's overture.

Kate began again. "We have sold a few of the diamonds we had, but, honestly, we didn't feel like we got a fair shake."

"Alright, let me tell you first up, I travel all over the world buying and selling gemstones. I have seen a lot of sellers get taken by buyers, particularly in Sri Lanka, and other places, too. If I don't buy anything from you, that's fine with me. I'll tell you what you have, but first, can you give me a little background on how you ended up with them? I can sense you have never dealt in diamonds before."

Kate felt a little more comfortable with Charlie and said, "Well, we dug a hole eighty feet deep in the Coocoran Opal Field below the Cretaceous and hit kimberlite, which, as you know, is the source rock for diamonds. Strange as it may seem, right there at that point were all of these diamonds, like a puff of smoke the earth gave up, pushing them up where we dug. What we found was all that there were. We didn't find any more. We did sell a few stones, but we felt we got taken."

"You have some spectacular uncut diamonds." Charlie pulled a jeweler's look from his pocket and began studying each stone individually. "These are some of the best stones I have seen in a long time. Just looking over all that you have on this table, and without giving them individual study, which should be done for a proper evaluation, I think you are looking at about one million dollars in uncut diamonds." Charlie looked up at Rusty and Kate, but he did not sense any surprise from what he had just told them. "You don't seemed surprised?" said Charlie.

"Well, we found these over five years ago," said Kate. "We sold a couple of stones then, but we got scared off by what this one jeweler told us. He said that it is almost impossible to sell uncut diamonds without papers. What he called the Kimberley process."

"Yes, that is true. There are few people today that will handle uncut diamonds without proper paperwork. I buy your story about where these diamonds are from. I wouldn't mind buying some of them, but I, like others, can't give you their full value." He looked at Rusty and Kate to see what they wanted to do.

"Look, Charlie, we admit we're out of our element on where to go with these stones," said Kate, thinking neither Rusty nor she had anything invested in them, since they dug them up from old Jaruk, who they found dead in his cabin over five years earlier. "Which ones do you want, and what will you pay?"

Charlie pulled five stones from both piles on the table. "Alright, this is the best I can do, and I understand your situation. I buy all kinds of stones all over the world like this. I know you want cash and no check. Am I correct?"

Rusty was the first to speak up this time. "You got that right, mate!"

Charlie took one more look at each stone, seeing them shining in the sun coming in the hotel windows. "I'll give you fifty thousand dollars in cash for these ten stones. That's my first and final offer. You can take it or leave it," Charlie said with little emotion.

Kate spoke first this time. "Alright, you got yourself a deal."

Charlie got up from where he was sitting and went to the vault that each room in the hotel had for valuables. He opened the vault, pulled out a small black satchel, and opened it with his back to Rusty and Kate. From the bag, he counted out fifty thousand dollars in hundred dollar bills. He closed the satchel and put it back in the vault, locking it before he turned around with the cash for Kate and Rusty.

He laid the money on the table. An enormous pile.

Since Charlie had taken five stones from each pile, there need not be any discussion as to how they split the money, so they each took half.

"It has been nice meeting you two. If you would like being my guests for the next hour, I'll take you into the private, wholesale gem and jewelry show that I came here to see that is going on down in the ballroom of this hotel. Then, before you leave, we might have a drink at the hotel's bar if you like?"

Again Rusty was the first to speak. "Hey, mate, we Australians are always up for a swig!"

"Alright then, I think we are done here. Let's go downstairs, and I'll show you into ballroom. They always welcome me, as I buy and sell to all the jewelers who have their work for sale there. Without me as your host, you could not get in. This show is not open to the public, although those who are registered members will bring in very wealthy people they know, trying to sell them their wares."

Charlie pulled out a small bag he was carrying in his pocket and tucked the ten stones into it. Kate and Rusty returned the remaining stones Charlie did not buy to their dirty brown bags and tucked them back in their pockets. Charlie looked around his room before leaving, making sure everything was secure.

Downstairs at the entrance to the ballroom stood two guards in black uniforms on either side of the door. Each had a metal detector wand in their hand. Charlie displayed his badge, which gave him entry to the ballroom.

"This gentleman and lady are my guests today," Charlie said to one of the guards.

Neither Rusty nor Kate had any guns with them; however, Rusty was carrying his twelve inch Bowie knife on his hip in a leather pouch.

"I'm sorry, sir, you will have to leave that knife with me if you wish to enter. You can have it back when you leave."

Rusty looked at the guard, blushed, handed him the knife, and said, "Sorry, we mates in the bush don't go anywhere without our knives."

The guard grinned and took Rusty's knife.

Charlie had already been in the ballroom earlier and showed both Kate and Rusty each exhibitor's display. In total, there were only twelve jewelers showing material, but given the amount of gems and jewels there, the room was full. While both Kate and Rusty had been in many jewelry stores in Sydney, the displays before them were unbelievable. They didn't know which way to look.

Charlie motioned Kate and Rusty to follow him to one display. There in the middle of the case was a spectacular 15 carat black opal surrounded by 1 carat diamonds with intermittent dark blue sapphires. Even Kate, who usually didn't show great emotion, stood there looking at the broach with her mouth open.

"Charlie, that is an outstanding Lightning Ridge black opal, as you probably know. That's the kind of stone we keeping searching for, but seldom see. They are so rare. When we hit that kind of color, we just want to keep digging, looking for this kind of stone," said Kate.

"Yeah, Charlie, that is a special stone," said Rusty. "The wholesale price on this piece is one hundred and fifty thousand dollars. I think you can see other gems, including opal, which you are familiar with. Look,

I'll give you about fifteen minutes to look around, and then I think we need to go have that drink."

Kate and Rusty could have stayed there all afternoon. They had made a deal with Charlie Keuper and were still thinking about all the cash they had in their pockets.

The three left the room. Rusty got his Bowie knife back, and they walked into the hotel bar.

"Alright, folks, my treat. What will it be?"

Both Kate and Rusty ordered a schooner of Tooheys beer. Charlie ordered a gin and tonic with a twist of lime.

"Well, it's been a pleasure. Let's drink up. I'm sorry to cut it short, but I have another meeting with a couple of the jewelers in that ballroom. That's what I came to Sydney for. Tomorrow, I leave for Hong Kong and plan to meet with a pearl manufacturer."

They finished their drinks and said their goodbyes. "Well, Rusty, let's get out of this town. I think it's back to Katoomba for the night and dinner at the Boomerang Café." "Fair dinkum, Kate."

CHAPTER 16

PETER GRANT AND HIS ASSISTANT

Hello. Is this Mr. Grant? My name is Rusty. I'm from Lightning Ridge, Australia. I was told to contact you regarding some uncut diamonds my mate and

I found here in Australia."

"You're calling from where?" inquired Peter Grant. "Lightning Ridge, Australia," repeated Rusty.

"Well, what do you want of me? I'm here in Las Vegas.

Seems to me that's a long way from home."

"Your name was given to me as someone who buys and sell gemstones," said Rusty.

"Yes, yes I do. Do you plan to be in Las Vegas? What is it again you have for sale?" inquired Peter.

"My mate here in Australia and I have some very nice uncut diamonds we would like to show you," said Rusty.

"Well, are you planning a trip to the States?" inquired

Peter.

"No, but is there somewhere we could meet in Australia?"

"I do travel all over the world looking for gemstones. As a matter of fact, next month, I have to meet a fellow in Brisbane, Queensland, regarding some sapphires he wants to sell me. Could we meet then? I will only be there for two days, and then I fly to Singapore," said Peter.

"Yes, that will do. What days will you be there?"

"It will be March fifth and sixth at the North Brisbane Lapidary Gem and Jewelry Festival. It's only two days. I would, however, hope to have everything done on the fifth. Look, that's a long way off. I will be spending the whole day there at the show on the fifth. It would be best if we meet there. I will have this number with me. When we meet, if I am tied up with someone, I will have my assistant there at the show with me. Her name is Sandy Reynolds. She is a certified gemologist, and she can talk to you about your diamonds. I'll also give you the name of the hotel we will be staying at, in case we are not at the show. It is the Hilton Brisbane on Elizabeth Street."

"Thanks. My mate's name is Kate. We are both bush people. I'm sure you can pick us out of a crowd," laughed Rusty.

"Look everyone has to be register to get into this gem and mineral show. If you inquire at the registration desk, I am sure someone can find us. Alright, I hope to see you and what you wish to sell." With that, Peter hung up the phone. Rusty called Kate right away. "Hey, Kate, I got that other American fellow. He said he can meet up in Brisbane next month."

"What! Do you realize how far that is? Some of that is on dirt road cross-country. That's a three day trip! Couldn't you get him to come somewhere closer?"

"Look, Kate, I'm just glad he talked to me at all." "Alright, maybe then, if you sell some of you diamonds in Brisbane, you can get yourself a new ute. I can see I'll have to drive again."

"Well, Kate, if we sell the rest of our diamonds, isn't that worth it?"

"Fair dinkum. We'll have to load up with extra tires and water. I don't want to get out in any of that country and have a flat tire. We'll have to pack a tent and provisions for camping. We'll have to come across the Gwydr Highway to Moree. I think we should stay the night there. To push on to Lemmon Tree Flats near Texas is just too far. We can get there the second day. Lots of cross country in that part of the woods. After Lemon Tree Flats, we can get on the Bruxner Highway, go through Lismore, and on to the Pacific Highway to Brisbane."

"I don't know, Kate, if I have ever made that trip," said Rusty.

"It's been years since I've been to Brisbane. When are we to meet this fellow?"

"On the fifth of next month. He said he would probably only be there one day."

"One day! Well, our trip for sure is three days. And we won't get there until the end of the third day. Where did he say he was staying?" inquired Kate.

"He said at the Hilton Brisbane on Elizabeth Street." "Well, he picked the fanciest hotel in town. We better look for a campsite outside of Brisbane. I'm not staying in a place like that. You know I don't like big cities." "Yes, Kate, I am well aware of that," said Rusty.

* * *

Three days before they were to meet with Peter Grant, they started out on their trip. This time of year, it was still summer in that part of Australia. It was hot and the roads were dusty. Because of the dust, they couldn't drive too fast. Because of the dirt they kicked up, any vehicle traveling in either direction could be seen for miles. In the area, the first day they had to be on the lookout for emus and kangaroos, who might jet out from the side of the road.

That day, they couldn't wait to get to Moree, their first stop. Kate's ute had no air-conditioning. This was a facility for travelers with camp units; however, there were small cabins people could rent if they weren't parking a camping van. They found the first camp, pulled in, and got a room. Once checked in, both Rusty and Kate went straight to the public facilities where they could get a shower. Kate carried a small charcoal cooking unit. They cooked up a meal from the stores they carried with them. Both were exhausted. Very little was said. They went straight to bed after cleaning their cooking utensils.

* * *

The following day, they were up by 6:00 and on the road, having warmed up a thermos of coffee and eaten a couple of cold sausage rolls. They made good time from Moree to Lemon Tree Flats and were there by 5:00 P.M.

This is one of the largest camp grounds in all of Australia with excellent camping facilities. The camp's grounds are so large they extend to both Queensland and New South Wales.

Kate and Rusty set up their individual tents, as there were no permanent sleeping facilities. There was an open shelter with a wood burning pit for cooking and heat should it be cold. However, that night, it was very hot with little movement of air. They shared the cooking area under the shelter with other travelers, which was the custom. Since it was dry, mosquitoes were not a problem; however, the tiny black flies were so thick, they were driving everyone crazy. They got in their noses, their eyes, their ears, and nothing made them go away. Both Kate and Rusty quickly ate their meals and got into their individual tents on the ground. While it was terribly hot, they at least had mesh fly nets to keep out the flies, which provided some comfort.

Because of the heat, Kate and Rusty were up by 5:00

A.M. and on their way down the road. The air had cooled off at that time of the morning, and the flies didn't seem to be as big a menace, even though it was still very hot. Before they camped for the night in Moree, Kate had filled her ute with diesel fuel. On their third day, Kate filed up her ute with diesel at Tenterfield before proceeding to Brisbane.

Near Glen Innes, they climbed up and over the Dividing Range and through the eucalyptus forests on their way to the Pacific Coast. As they went east, the temperature dropped by thirty degrees. Once they reached the Pacific Highway, Kate and Rusty felt the Pacific Ocean breezes against their faces.

It was about 4:30 P.M. on the outskirts of Brisbane. Kate saw a camper park ahead and pulled in. It was similar to the one where they stayed in Moree. They each got separate small cottages. This park also had public showers. After Kate and Rusty showered and felt renewed again, they traveled another half mile down the road to the Emu Park Café where they had dinner before returning to the camper park.

* * *

The next day, Kate and Rusty drove into Brisbane, parked in the Elizabeth Street parking garage, and walked the half-block to the Brisbane Hilton, where Peter Grant was waiting for them outside.

"Welcome to Brisbane," he said, smiling.

"I've been here before," Kate said. "Let's get this done."

She walked into the hotel ahead of Peter and Rusty.

Peter widened his eyes at Rusty. Rusty shrugged. They followed Kate into the lobby.

"Where's your room?" Kate asked, heading to the elevator.

"907."

They entered the elevator and Kate pushed the button. They rode up to the room in silence, except for the rustle of Peter's pants as he dug for the room key.

In the suite, the curtains were pulled back, revealing buildings glistening in the sun. Rusty walked over to the window and, looking at an angle, he could see the Brisbane River, glistening to rival the thousands of windows rising from the streets below him.

"Some place you got here," Rusty said.

"I like it," Peter said. "Stay here every time I make it to this part of the world."

"There's no better part," Rusty said, smiling. Peter smiled. "Come to L.A. I'll show—"

Kate huffed loudly, dropped her satchel of diamonds on the table in the middle of the room, and sat down.

Peter Grant looked annoyed. "As I was saying, I'll show you a part of the world to rival this one."

"Maybe I'll take you up on that, if you give me enough for my diamonds," Rusty said.

Kate scowled at him, or at least he thought she scowled. Her face looked like that most of the time, so it was hard to know for sure.

"You gals can chit-chat after we finish up," Kate said. She pointed to her satchel on the table. "Rusty, put yours there. Peter, see what we got."

Peter pulled a cloth from his pants pocket and laid it on the table. Rusty carefully poured his diamonds on the table. Peter then poured Kate's diamonds from her satchel.

"Sandy, the gemologist who works with me, should be here shortly," Peter said, just as there was a knock on the door. "Must be her now."

He walked to the door, which was hidden from the rest of the room by a partition.

Kate covered the diamonds with the edges of the cloth.

"Keep quiet," she said to Rusty.

Rusty nodded and looked out the window.

"I thought I had the wrong room," Rusty overheard Sandy say to Peter. "So quiet I couldn't hear anything on the other side of the door."

Rusty turned to see Peter walk from behind the partition and look at Kate, who sat looking in the other direction. "No fun and games here," Peter said.

An instant later, Sandy walked from behind the partition.

Rusty stepped back, blinked. "Huh?" he said. "What?" Peter said.

Rusty looked at him. "Huh?" he said. "Did you say something?" Peter said.

"Um, no, nothing," Rusty said. He couldn't take his eyes off Sandy, but not because she was beautiful, which she was, but because she so closely resembled his ex-wife.

"Hello," Sandy said, reaching out her hand to Rusty.

Rusty hesitated, then extended his hand. "Rusty," he said. Uncanny resemblance to Lil, he thought.

Peter turned to Kate. "Sandy, this is Kate," Peter said. "Nice to meet you, Kate," Sandy said, extending her hand.

Kate nodded, but didn't offer her hand. "You going to tell me how much these are worth?" Kate said and pulled the cloth back from the diamonds.

"You have quite a collection there," Sandy said.

Kate nodded.

Rusty said nothing, only continued to study the side of Sandy's face. *Besides the height difference,* he thought, *Sandy could be my ex-wife from twenty years ago, back when we were both young and in love, when Lightning Ridge had all either of us needed.*

"Rusty?" Peter said. "You want to sit?"

He looked around to see Peter and Sandy were already sitting with Kate. Kate was scowling at him. At least he thought she was scowling…

He sat and looked at Sandy once more before willing himself to focus on Peter.

As Peter and Sandy began to sort through the diamonds, Rusty shuffled through the earliest memories he had of himself and Lilly, Lil, he called her.

"Why don't I just call you Lil," he had said to her when they first met **over twenty years ago** *outside the 'Roo in the Moon bar. A friend of a friend had set them up on a blind date, and this is where they chose to meet, outside a dirty, nearly forgotten bar on the outskirts of Lightning Ridge.*

"And why do you think you should call me Lil?" she had said, stepping close and smiling up at him.

"'Cause you're little," he had said, smiling.

"And why should I let you call me little?" she said, stepping closer.

"Because you are," he had said, stepping closer to her. "Oh, really?" she said, still smiling up at him.

While she had him off guard with her smile, she grabbed his hand quickly and bent his thumb back hard, not letting go as he dropped to his knees. "Who's li'l now?" she said, laughing.

It hurt so bad he had to laugh, too. "OK. OK," he said. "I'm li'l."

She smiled and let go of his thumb.

He stood slowly, regaining his breath. "Wouldn't have hurt, but that thumb's bad from an old opal mining injury," he said.

"Oh, really?" she said, reaching quickly for his other thumb. He was quick this time and pulled back. "Yeah, me and a couple buddies back there," he said, turning to look westward into the Outback, glowing red with the setting sun. "We got this idea—"

"I got an idea," Lil said, taking hold of his arm and turning him around. "I got an idea you ought to kiss me."

Rusty smiled. "I don't kiss my friends," he said.

"I'm not your friend," she said, stepping even closer to him. "We just met a minute ago," Rusty said, still smiling, but speaking without a smile in his voice.

"We weren't friend when we met, and we're not friends now," she said. "So kiss me."

She rose onto her toes, stretched upwards and leaned into him. He turned his head and lips down to hers. They kissed softly. She was the first to pull away, leaving him wanting more. He leaned forward and down, but she pulled further away.

Now he remembered that's how it always went with her: She was always the first to pull away, and she kept pulling further away, all the way to Sydney, far away from Lightning Ridge and the opal mines she hated so much.

What would she think of me now, he thought, *sitting in the Brisbane Hilton, splitting diamonds with Kate and a rich American and a woman who looked like the version of her from twenty years ago?*

She could be here now if she hadn't kept pulling away, but, really, how could he blame her? He had never committed to anything more than the day at hand, but despite living for the day, he had always wanted to be more than just an opal miner and a kismet-man whose swagger outweighed his smarts.

But who am I trying to fool? Myself? he thought. He looked around the room and then down at his dirty, faded jeans and old boots. As he half-listened to the others haggle over the worth of the diamonds, he knew that no amount of diamond trading or fancy suites in big hotels would get the opal out of his blood.

But as for the swagger, well, he thought he could live without that. Long ago it had somehow led him to Lil, and most recently it had led him to Milla. Or was it the kismet that led them to him? *Either way,* he thought, *I see the damage it has done. Left me with an ex-wife, two kids I never see, a destroyed ute in my front yard at Mulga's Rush, and, possibly, my name on some Serbian hit-list in Sydney.*

Kate suddenly rose from the table, pulling him from his thoughts. "No way his are better than mine," she said to Peter, while pointing at Rusty.

"I'm afraid they are, Kate," Peter said. "Now do you want to have a seat, and let's finish this up?"

Kate walked around the room, mumbling to herself. She never once looked out of the window to admire the view.

Sandy turned to Rusty. "You look familiar," she said. "Huh?" Rusty said. "Me?"

"Yeah, you," Sandy said and smiled. "You ever go to the States?"

"Never been there," Rusty said. "Peter said I should go." "This all goes OK," Sandy said, looking at Kate, "you come to the States and see me, and I'll figure out where I've seen you before."

"It's a deal," Rusty said, extending his hand to Sandy.

Sandy raised her hand from her lap, accidentally striking the table hard enough to rattle the diamonds. She took Rusty's hand awkwardly and shook.

In the corner of the room, Kate wheeled around, pulled from her thoughts by the knock of Sandy's hand against the table.

"I walk away for a minute," Kate said and walked quickly back to the table. "If you're buying his, you might as well buy mine. We don't know nothing about diamonds anyway." Kate extended her hand to Peter.

"No. Now wait, Kate," Peter said, waving her off.

"This is how I do it," Kate said, holding her arm out. "Just a handshake. No papers."

"Kate," Rusty said, rising from the table.

"You keep quiet," Kate said to Rusty, not turning her gaze from Peter. "You shake on this, Grant."

Peter looked at Sandy, who shrugged. He looked at Rusty, who also shrugged, then nodded his head to indicate that he might as well shake, Kate wasn't going anywhere.

"OK, Kate," Peter said, shaking Kate's hand.

"I'll wait over there while you get our cash," Kate said, walking to the window, finally at least pretending to admire the view.

Peter walked to the room safe.

"Wow," Sandy said.

"Once she makes up her mind, she doesn't change it," Rusty said. "But she's usually right not to, and I'm glad for that." He scratched the back of his neck, and thought of how Kate's plan to split up the diamonds eventually got him here. "She got a poor opal miner to the Hilton in Brisbane to make more money than he's had in his whole life," he said. "So I trust her on about everything these days."

A minute later, Peter Grant returned from the safe with the money, split the money between Kate and Rusty in accordance with the quality of each of their diamonds, and scooped the diamonds into a tiny felt bag, which he then took to the safe.

Kate stuffed her cash where she could, walked to the door, opened it, and without looking at Rusty, said, "You coming?"

"You go," Rusty said. "I'll see you in the Ridge."

Kate walked out, letting the door slam shut behind her. "Pleasant woman," Peter mumbled.

Sandy laughed then looked at Rusty. "You want to grab lunch?" Sandy said, standing.

"I would," Rusty said, standing with Sandy. "But not today."

Sandy looked disappointed.

"I'm ute hunting," he said. "Then heading back to Lightning Ridge."

Peter approached Sandy and Rusty. He offered Rusty his hand. "Pleasure doing business," he said.

Rusty shook Peter's hand, then offered his hand to Sandy. "When I come to the States, I'll look you up," he said, smiling.

Sandy smiled and shook his hand. She pulled a business card from a small purse she had sat under her chair. "Here's my card so you can find me," she said.

Rusty took it and smiled. "Now if you'll excuse me, I have a ute to buy," he said, stuffing cash into his boots and the front pockets of his pants. When he was finished, he touched the brim of his hat and quickly made his way out the door.

* * *

Two hours later, Brisbane was in Rusty's review mirror.

Amazing how a wad of cash can speed things up, he thought. He immediately thought of Lil and how quickly their marriage had fallen apart. *Guess a wad of cash would have just sped that up, too.*

For a while he just drove, thinking of nothing but the road, passing the landmarks he and Kate had passed the day before when he could think of nothing but the money the diamonds would bring. When the sun touched the horizon, he thought of Milla driving Drago's car behind him into the darkness. He thought of what that must feel like, to know that you will never come back. He then thought of Jaruk slumped over his table, and he wondered if Jaruk had realized only moments before he reached the end that he was not coming back. He wondered, too, if in the last moments, the man had thought about his hoard of diamonds, buried and saved for a day that never came.

When the sun set and the stars twinkled into place, he found a wide spot on the side of the road and pulled over, and as he settled into his seat, getting as comfortable as he could get for the night, he thought again of Milla, sitting with her head leaned back against the edge of the Artesian Baths, gazing up to the stars, plotting who knows what. He then thought of Sue, sitting patiently beside him, always patiently beside him. He thought of her as if she were sitting beside him now. What would she think about his new ute? His wad of cash?

"Who are you trying to impress," she would say. "You," he would say.

"You're not," she would say. "Why?" he would say.

"Those things don't impress me," she would say.

He thought of something he would say.

Then he thought of something she would say.

Then he thought of what he would say and what she would say until he drifted off to sleep, smiling slightly.

* * *

Nearly two days later, when he finally arrived in Lightning Ridge, the sun was rising over the small town.

He drove slowly between

the squat buildings, turning left, then right, then left again until he reached the Blue Light Café.

Only three vehicles were in the parking lot— Max's, Sue's, and Kate's. He backed his ute into a parking space, turned off the engine, and went into the café. When he entered, Kate looked up from her coffee directly at him, and he took that as an invitation to join her.

"Where's Sue?" Rusty said.

"Helping Max," Kate said and sipped her coffee.

Rusty looked around, hoping Sue would come out soon. No matter how many times he sat silently with Kate, he never felt comfortable. When Sue finally did come out, she was carrying Kate's breakfast in one hand and a pot of coffee in another and was looking down, watching her footing on the recently mopped floor.

She was almost to the table before she looked up. When she saw Rusty, she eyed him suspiciously. "What are you doing sneaking in here?"

"Looking for you," he said.

Her face and shoulders relaxed, and she smiled slightly, crookedly, almost. She sat Kate's breakfast and the pot of coffee on the table. "What'll you have?" she asked, pulling her notepad from her apron.

"You don't need that," Rusty said. "Your usual, then?" Sue said.

"Kind of," Rusty said and glanced at Kate, who was so busy eating that she gave no indication that she even knew he and Sue were there.

"If this is your usual pickup line, I don't need it," Sue said, still smiling slightly.

"Then I won't give it to you, Sue," Rusty said, tapping the empty coffee cup in front of him. "No pickup lines, just coffee."

Sue poured the coffee, and she and Rusty smiled slightly at each other, as if sharing an inside joke.

"Anything else?" Sue asked.

"Whatever she had," Rusty said, pointing to Kate's half- empty plate. "Must be good."

"Is," Kate said, chewing her eggs.

Rusty watched Sue take his order to the kitchen. When he turned back around, Kate was chewing another mouthful of eggs and studying him.

"None of my business," Kate said, still chewing, "but you better get on with that."

Rusty knew she was talking about Sue, and although he had already made that decision himself, he found it oddly comforting that Kate had given her approval, her blessing, even, or as much a blessing as Kate could ever give to anything.

Kate took another bite of eggs, and as she chewed, she continued to study Rusty. The look in her eyes told him she had more advice, advice that he should listen hard to and try hard to follow.

She swallowed her eggs and pointed her fork at him. "One other thing, Rusty," Kate said, looking him square in the eyes. "Maybe you should go back to mining opals, and I'll go back to my sheep and cattle. Maybe that way, we can both stay out of trouble."

AUTHORS

Richard Holmes spent over 35 years in corporate America holding various financial management positions. He was a licensed certified public accountant during his corporate career and was instrumental in launching startup companies in both the mining and manufacturing industries. In retirement, he spends his time writing books both fiction and non-fiction that relate to the many ventures he has been involved with during his lifetime.

Randy Hughes lives in North Carolina with his lovely wife, Lori, their wonderful son, Dylan, their puppy, Roxy, and their very old cat, Daisy. He has had an interest in writing since he was young, which lead to a Master's Degree in Rhetoric and Composition from UNC Charlotte and a Bachelor's Degree in English from Coastal Carolina University. In his spare time, he enjoys reading, writing, and traveling with his family.

ILLUSTRATOR

Bryan Cook (a.k.a Boris) is a North Carolina-based artist with a breadth of talents and interests. In addition to the illustrations found within this novel, he has left his creative fingerprints all across the auto racing community. His use of vibrant colors, vigorous lines and dynamic perspectives, helps him capture the high energy and thrill of the fast- moving, four-wheeled vehicles that he loves.

The seeds of that love were planted when he was introduced to NASCAR when he was 12 years old. One of the very first sketches he created was of the No.18 Joe Gibbs Racing race car at Daytona Motor Speedway. Twelve years later Boris would begin working for Joe Gibbs Racing as Digital Marketing Director! He has also designed the paint schemes of over 20 race cars used in NASCAR races and other national series events.

His work is collected by prominent people and organizations in the auto racing community including Toyota, Dollar General, M&M'S/ Mars Inc., Target, Joe Gibbs Racing, and others. Additionally his portraiture has been published in USA Today and other national publications. You can find out more about Boris online @BorisArtwork and BorisCarArt.com

CPSIA information can be obtained
at www.ICGtesting.com
Printed in the USA
JSHW032121021221
20941JS00002B/46

9 781953 115607